"Surreal, dreamy and in-depth, *I Keep My Visions to Myself* is a vivid snapshot of just how lost an up-and-coming artist in their 20s can get in the dizzying chaos of today's world... A 2020s mashup of *High Fidelity* meets *Reality Bites*. Paralyzed by the trappings of early success, a young Los Angeles singer of a buzzworthy band floats along, unsure of where to go or what to do with her future besides drink and make questionable decisions. A terrifically relatable, sprawling adventure through the terrorscape of LA, and a book that grants creative freedom for all of us who feel directionless at times."

—Jessamyn Violet, author of *Secret Rules to Being a Rockstar*
+ drummer of Movie Club

"I resonated with Stevie so much. It made me fall in love with making music and the life I've chosen all over again. I didn't want to put it down. An inspiring and captivating read!"

—Chayla Hope, musician

"*I Keep My Visions to Myself* is a cathartic depiction of the existential spiral that comes with being a creative in today's industry. It does a great job of highlighting the self-destructive patterns that many of us go through and the liberatory nature of relationships and community."

—Connor Musarra, musician

"*The Day of the Locust* by Nathanial West and *Ask the Dust* by John Fante for the post-Covid world. A brutally realistic journey of a Los Angeles dreamer. The story of Stevie, a young woman who is on the cusp of success as a musician, but the possibility of this new success causes an existential crisis in her soul. Leading to visions and memories of her mother. Her team of friends, a poet named Claire and an Uber driver Door Dasher platonic buddy named Finn assist Stevie in understanding her crisis and coming to terms with her visions and fears. It is the kind of story where nothing really happens, but inside that nothing the biggest choices are being made."

—Noah Cicero, author of *The Human War*

"*I Keep My Visions To Myself* takes readers on a heady trip through the sun-baked streets of Los Angeles as they follow a young musician searching for her *raison d'être*."

—Matthew Binder, author of *Pure Cosmos Club*

I Keep My Visions to Myself

Mallory Smart

WITH AN

MMXXIII

This book is a work of fiction.

www.withanxbooks.com
Cover Design by Tori Huynh
Layout by Jon Nix
WAX007
ISBN 979-8-9874787-4-5

Most women would not be happy being me. People say, ‘But you’re alone.’ But I don’t feel alone. I feel very un-alone.

— **Stevie Nicks**

Prologue

FireBeat

Electric Stardust – "Whisper In The Wind"

NEW MUSIC **OCTOBER 14, 2022** 3:15 PM
BY **LENNY RIFFTER**

There's something special about discovering a new band and becoming an early fan. You get to watch them grow and evolve, cheering them on as they gain recognition and success. And that's exactly what's happening with Electric Stardust, a band that's quickly making a name for themselves thanks to their hit song *Whispers In The Wind*.

It all started a few years ago when a group of musicians came together in the little-known, small town of Los Angeles. The group had a collective love of classic rock and roll and art pop. But it wasn't until their lead singer, Stevie Fischer, wrote *Whispers In The Wind* that they hit it big.

The song is a mystical anthem with a chorus that lives in your head for days. It's the kind of song that you hear once and immediately want to listen to again. And that's exactly what happened when Electric Stardust played it at a local music festival I was attending in Echo Park.

The crowd went wild, and soon the song started to explode all over social media. Most notably TikTok due to one person's video of it going viral causing countless people to duet. People couldn't get enough of Electric Stardust and Whispers In The Wind. The band is slowly building a faithful fanbase, playing shows in almost every California venue you could think of, and have just been offered a deal to sign with a major record label.

Staying indie for now, they've decided to release their own self-produced debut album, also titled *Whispers In The Wind*, which was released to critical acclaim. It contains a variety of songs that highlight the band's range, with a mixture of baller rock anthems like *Electric Nights* and ethereal ballads like *Broken Dreams*.

But it's *Whispers In The Wind* that remains the band's biggest hit. The song has been streamed millions of times on Spotify, and the band has even performed it on national TV shows.

Part of the song's appeal is its ethereal vocals and mystical approach towards love. In the face of haunting realities, it's important to keep pushing forward and never give up on your heart's desire. And that's exactly what Electric Stardust is doing.

There is high demand for a national tour from their fans, so they could bring their once-in-a-generation sound to the masses.

It's hard to say what the future holds for Electric Stardust. But one thing can't be overstated: they've made a lasting impression in the wide world of music with Stevie Fischer's hit single *Whispers In The Wind*. As for the band's loyal following, there's no doubt that the band will have more electrifying music to come.

In a press release, Stevie Fischer says how the song came together:

> *Whispers In The Wind* is a song that encapsulated the power of resilience and dreams, born from my early days as a songwriter. I first came up with the idea for the song during a challenging period in my life when I could only find solace in music. After long discussions with our drummer, Dustin Evy, we booked a studio in Silverlake for him to record the synth and drum beats that became the basis of the song. He shared those initial recordings with the rest of the band who became increasingly motivated to create a true identity for this album. Julie, our lead guitarist, began arranging materials the second she heard the track, and I dove into crafting the lyrics. Eventually, it just emerged into one cohesive sound that we wanted to serve as a reminder for all of us to trust in the whispers of the universe and to persevere.

Don't do anything at all

In a strange, otherworldly version of Echo Park, the streets are lined with trees that glow with eerie, neon lights, and the air thick with the sound of ethereal music. She walks down the street and sees people dancing in the shadows, their bodies moving in hypnotic, psychical ways.

She approaches a small, dimly lit dive that closely resembles a place that she'd passed by many times on her way to work: Monte Carlo Bar. She hears a voice calling out to her. Above her are figures standing on the roof of the bar, beckoning her to come closer. Stevie reflexively climbs stairs that seem to just appear, and she moves even farther away from the neon-lit trees, feeling a sense of both anticipation and unease. As she got closer, she realized that the roof was actually a makeshift stage and looked down to see the superlunary figures, looking up in a daze. They were an audience in a trance waiting for something. Maybe they were even waiting on her. She could see her band, Electric Stardust, was. They were huddled with their instruments on stage, looking coldly in her direction, ready for her to finally join them so they could play to the hypnotic horde below.

But as soon as her small feet crept onto what she thought was a stage, everything began to fall apart. The bodies that once moved as celestial beings disappear, the music turns to static, and her bandmates vanish into thin air like puffs of smoke. Stevie is alone on a dark roof, with nothing but her fear and anxiety.

A creature approaches from the shadows of the roof and introduces itself as the guardian of the dreamscape and tells Stevie that she can be given the power to help save her life from a great darkness that threatens to consume her. The creature comes closer, cloaked in white, like a goddess from another realm, and gives Stevie a small, glowing orb that supposedly contains the power of the moon, telling her that it is the key to saving her life, the universe, and everything.

As Stevie takes the orb, she feels a surge of energy coursing through her body, but as she gazes out at the cold and dark street, she suddenly feels a strange sensation wash over her. Like a gust of wind, but instead of blowing through her, it blew into her, filling her up with a sense of dread.

She reaches for the Xanax that she typically carries in her pocket only to find an empty bottle. In a panic, she runs down to what she thinks is Monte Carlo Bar but lands in a labyrinthine maze instead. The walls are made of twisted metal and seem to pulse with metaphysical energy as if they were coming alive just to swallow her and her life's ambitions all at the same time. Every step she takes feels heavy like she's wading through dense, unidentifiable muck, and she can hear even more strange whispers and echoes all around her now.

Suddenly, she sees a glimmer of neon light up ahead, and she starts to run toward it. The faster she runs, the more the neon lights flicker and dance in the midnight air, and she realizes with horror that it's actually a swarm of fireflies. As they surround her, their wings beat faster and faster until they start to burn, and Stevie becomes enveloped in a blinding inferno.

A car alarm vibrates through the air. With each second it gets louder and suddenly Stevie wakes up drenched in sweat and panting. Her room is silent, but she can still hear the echoes of the dream all around her. She shivers, feeling like something cold and slimy is crawling up her spine. It takes her a few moments to catch her breath and remind herself that it was just a dream, but the feeling of unease lingers long after she's calmed down.

Stevie sat up in a twin sized bed, her heart still racing from the intensity of the dream. She took a few heavy breaths, trying to calm herself down, and then looked at her Apple watch to check her heart rate. It was high enough for a normal person to call a doctor, but not high enough to make Stevie truly care. She picked up her iPhone 12 beside her bed. Whenever Stevie had wild and bizarre dreams she put them down in her notes app before she could forget them. You never know what can inspire you later on in life or just make you laugh when times are hard.

Now fully awake at only 12 am, she scrolled through her Twitter. Her friend Finn DM'd her a few hours earlier. Stevie's goal that year was to set boundaries and live a more balanced life so she told herself she wouldn't respond until morning. But now with her eyes unable to close and with the knowledge that she'd be tossing around the rest of the night, she messaged him back. Stevie and Finn had known each other for almost a decade but she still wasn't entirely sure how they actually met. She knew they were both in high school at the time but they lived in different places. He lived in West Hollywood and she lived in Inland Empire. It was clearly through some social media platform but she just couldn't figure out which. It was 2022 and they were always on Twitter, so whichever platform was big in 2012 is where it likely happened. But it didn't really matter at this point. Somehow, the two of them found each other living in the same area after high school and had gone through almost everything together ever since.

When she clicked into his message she saw that he weirdly wanted to know if she wanted to join him on a DoorDash run. He was always switching between gig economy jobs. Uber, Lyft, UberEats, DoorDash, and Instacart. He recently got kicked off Uber because he responded to a text message during a ride. Finn insisted it was only that one time but Stevie knew that Uber would've given him the benefit of the doubt if it was a one-time thing.

"Hey," she typed, her fingers shaking slightly. "Are you still Dashing?"

A few seconds later, Finn's reply appeared on the screen. "Nah, slow night. It's why I messaged. We could've hung if it got lame but whatever. What's up?"

Stevie took a deep breath and then began to type out the details of her dream, describing the labyrinthine bar, the whispers, and the feeling of being trapped. As she wrote, she could feel her pulse quickening again, and she knew that she was reliving the fear and confusion of the dream. She heavily considered going to her bathroom to grab a Xanax but decided she'd just throw on *Lord Of The Rings* instead, hoping that she'd crash eventually from watching it.

When she finished typing out her reply, she hit send and waited for Finn's response. The entire intro of *The Fellowship of the Ring* had gone by: *"One ring to rule them all. One ring to find them. One ring to bring them all and in the darkness bind them."* No response. She should've known. Her dream was too weird. She wouldn't respond if she got a message like that. So she turned the volume up on her shitty MacBook Air so she could focus on the film and not the weird dream. But the more she watched, the more she related to Frodo. He was just a mere halfling caught up in something he didn't ask for. She was just a 26 yr old caught up in something she didn't ask for. Both of them having to clean up a mess that someone in their family made. It was too real. Like her dream.

Finally, her phone lit up again.

"Wow, that's weird as fuck," Finn wrote back. "Are you freaking because you think it means something?"

Stevie thought about it for a moment and then typed back. "I don't know. It just felt so real, you know? Like I was actually there. Maybe it's a sign. Maybe I'm feeling trapped in my life right now, and everything keeping me steady is slowly slipping away."

Stevie considered this for a moment and then took in a deep sigh of relief. She probably just needed to get that out of her head. Put the burden of her irrational fears onto someone else. But Finn always had a way of cutting through the bullshit and getting straight to the heart of the matter.

"Fuck off," he wrote back. "You need to start thinking of your life as something you chose and not something that was forced on you. Besides, the dream probably didn't mean shit. It's a full moon."

"The fuck does that mean," she asked.

"IDK, all my chick friends say moon cycles do something to sleep. It's a full moon. It's probably just throwing you off or some shit. Look it up and chill out. I'm gonna try Dashing again. Maybe other people are fucked up because of the moon and will order now," he said.

"K," she wrote back, disheartened.

As she put her phone down her screen lit up one more time.

"Just be chill. It's just gonna be a long night and then it'll be over. Watch something boring and maybe you'll crash. Gnight."

Stevie looked at the screen for a while before laying back in bed and felt a sense of calm washing over her. She wasn't crazy. It was just the moon. Fuck the moon. She could barely see it through her bedroom window because of the light pollution but flicked it off anyways. Picked up her Apple Remote and dwelled on whether *Lord of the Rings* was boring enough for her to fall asleep to. She sighed and put on *Star Wars Episode I: The Phantom Menace* instead. She had work in the morning and needed all the sleep she could possibly get.

Your opiate is the

air that you breathe

Stevie arrived at her day job at the record store, Vinyl Haven, early in the morning, half ready for her shift and half ready to pass out from lack of sleep. As soon as she walked in, she could hear a gaggle of her coworkers laughing and picking on each other in the back room. She headed over to the counter and saw that the owner, Jack, was already there, probably writing down inventory on an old ledger that he never would throw away. She'd joke that he should join the 21st century and he'd respond in some grumbling way. It was their thing. But she was far too tired to even interact with him.

With each step she made into the store she slowly felt a sense of comfort and belonging wash over her. The familiar scent of vinyl and old paper sleeves. The vintage posters on the walls. She couldn't help but always be reminded of all of her favorite musicians and bands. The gods and goddesses in her life. She soaked in the natural light that poured in through the large windows, which cast a warm glow on the store's cozy interior, even though the sunlight still hurt her eyes from lack of sleep.

As she made her way through the aisles, Stevie admired the rows of vinyl records, sorted meticulously by genre, artist, and era. She felt a sense of pride and satisfaction with the organized chaos of the store's eclectic selection. A hallmark that made this 40-year-old store so popular. The warm mustard yellow walls with their retro vibe and floor-to-ceiling shelves of music only made it better.

"Hey Stevie, how's it be?" Jack asked, finally looking up from his ledger.

"Good, thanks. Ready for another day at the store," Stevie replied, trying to sound more awake and not like the zombie that she felt like she was inside. On mornings like this, she'd typically grab a coffee before work and down it on the way to the store. She knew to never bring a drop of coffee into Vinyl Haven. Never there. No drinks allowed.

"Great. So, did you hear about that guy who came in yesterday asking for Green Day?" Jack said with a smirk.

Stevie cringed inwardly, knowing that this was the start of another one of Jack's music taste rants. She had grown used to the way he and her coworkers would make fun of customers' musical preferences behind their backs. It didn't sit well with her, but she wanted desperately to seem like one of them: an anti-establishment music lover who thought all mainstream things were crap.

"Yeah, I heard. Can't believe anyone would listen to that shit," Stevie said, trying to sound serious.

Her severely uptight coworker, Claire, scoffed, "Seriously if Green Day was ever badass it was in their early punk days in the '90s. Now they just sound like Dad Rock."

"I don't know, American Idiot was pretty lit," Ben chimed in gleefully as he focused on his work.

Claire immediately struck back with, "Yeah, it was pretty lit for a corporate mainstream band that wanted to seem relevant again by hitting at an institution it already knew we all hated..."

"Damn, you cold," Ben laughed and walked away

to do other things. "Guess we're all gonna pretend that Billie Joe Armstrong wasn't everyone's '90s crush... aside from Kurt Cobain."

Claire groaned and rolled her eyes.

"Bro, I legit thought people had better taste in an area like this. Seriously, next thing I know one of you is going to say you think Dave Matthews was a snack."

Ben laughed more, clearly enjoying goading Claire on.

Claire always gave Stevie bad vibes. It's not like they ever had shitty interactions with each other, but ever since Claire joined the "Vinyl Haven Family" the air of negativity in the store seemed to increase. The chick constantly dissed everyone's taste in music. Stevie couldn't tell if Claire meant to be that way, but she just had an air of superiority about her that made Stevie feel small and lame for not having such "refined" music tastes.

When Stevie dissed Green Day, Stevie felt a pang of guilt. She knew that some of her friends dug Green Day, and she herself had even been to a concert of theirs at Hollywood Bowl a few years ago. But she just kept quiet and focused on getting to work. Claire threw a Circle Jerks record on and Stevie went to the back room to get the box of new records for her to organize. As she flipped through the stacks of arrivals to be stocked, the scent of musty cardboard enveloped her, transporting her back to a time when physical albums were the norm. It was slightly sweet and acidic, with a hint of dustiness that was a testament to the records' age and history. She took one out of the bin and handed it to Claire to throw on the turntable next when Circle Jerks was done. Stevie never looked at what record she was grabbing. She closed her eyes and just picked. Just another one of the games to keep work interesting when things at the store were slow.

And there it was: Fleetwood Mac. A subtle hint of warm plastic filled the air, as the grooves on the vinyl made contact with the needle. Without fail, it was Rumours. The only album by a mainstream band that was deemed acceptable by the rest of her coworkers. It was, after all, a classic. But for Stevie, it was something more—a time capsule.

She became lost in thought as she flipped through the records at the store, barely paying attention to anything else that was happening around her. The sound of Fleetwood Mac's "Dreams" came on over the speakers. The song took her back to her childhood, to a time when her mother was still sane and they would listen to the same album together. Her mom twirling like the "White Witch" while drinking wine that she'd inevitably spill. A young Stevie admiring her with childlike wonder as she looked up at her from the floor. Eventually, her mom would grab her up to twirl like some mystical goddess until they both would get dizzy and collapse on their sofa that her mom found at some thrift shop, laughing.

Her mother was a huge fan of Stevie Nicks and that weird as fuck woman even named her after the iconic singer. They listened to the same Fleetwood Mac album on repeat, to the point where Stevie memorized every word of every song and imagined herself becoming another famous Stevie.

She felt a wave of remorse as she thought about how much her mother had counted on her daughter becoming a "White Witch" someday. Stevie was in a band named Electric Stardust and played live, but she never had any real urge to be famous. She didn't care. She was content. The mere act of performing was enough for her, but the thought of that was unacceptable to her mother. The woman grew more and more unstable with each day until she lost her touch with reality completely. Too much alcohol and mental illness will do that to a person. Her mom would never be famous and her daughter strangely had no desire to be famous. And the world her mother knew would just continue spinning right 'round the sun like a vinyl record slowly fading out until nothing remained and nobody would truly know who she was.

The thought of this unsettled Stevie so much that she felt an irrational need to escape a place where she always felt at home. She grabbed the Fleetwood Mac album from the turntable and shelved it while she made her way to the front of the store to take a break. As she approached the counter, Ben was already there, leaning on the counter and scrolling through his phone. Jack was probably in his office which was really just a really big closet with old posters and Christmas lights that he strung up. In a way, it reminded her of the office that Moe revealed in the back of his tavern in that one *Simpsons* episode where he trained Homer to be a boxer. Small, dank, and full of nostalgia. Stevie sensed that Jack at one point was MUCH more involved in the indie music scene than he was now.

"Hey, Stevie..." Ben hummed her name out while looking up from his phone. "You taking a break too?"

Stevie nodded and leaned on the counter he was at. "Yeah, I need some coffee."

Ben chuckled. "Don't we all?" He grabbed his red flannel jacket and they both headed out the door. They both looked back at Claire who had gone into the stock room to handle what they should've been doing but neither seemed to care. Hopefully, she'd figure out that she should go to the front and man the counter now that they were both gone.

The sun was shining brightly outside, and the warmth felt good on Stevie's skin. As someone who lived primarily at night, this was a rare feeling. They walked down the street to a nearby coffee shop, chatting about their favorite albums and the upcoming record releases they were both excited about. The coffeeshop was dimly-lit. The walls were painted a shade of red that made Stevie think about *Twin Peaks*, and the only light came from the Edison bulbs hanging from above. The smell of freshly brewed coffee and burnt sugar filled the air. This was the kind of atmosphere she was more accustomed to.

As they passed the time in line and waited for their gentrified coffee, Stevie couldn't help but feel grateful for Ben's company. He was one of the few people at work that she genuinely enjoyed spending time with, and their conversations always left her feeling uplifted. A wave of calm always washed over her in Ben's presence. He was one of only a handful of people she worked with that she could talk to about music without feeling like a poser.

As she got her hazelnut latte, she shook off her feelings about her mother and focused on the present moment. She was young, living in LA, working at a record store, and surrounded by music and the kind of friends she never could've imagined having when she was younger. Boomers probably would've called them "wasters" or "hipsters" but all they really were just people in their 20s being true to themselves and not postponing their happiness until retirement. Life was good for them and she wasn't going to let memories or expectations ruin her day.

Once Ben got his drink, a red-eye coffee, they found a table outside and sat down. She regretted not looking at the menu long enough to see that the coffeeshop had that. She'd only had it a few times with Finn, but she knew it would've immediately energized her. Instead, her latte's caffeine level only nudged her toward a small bit of happiness.

"So, what are you doing after work today?" Ben asked, taking a sip of the coffee she wished she had.

Stevie shrugged. "Not sure yet. Maybe check out a show later or something."

"Nice," he said, smiling. "You always know the best places to go. Looking for anyone to join you?"

Stevie choked on her coffee when he asked this, knowing that she had no real intention of going out. "Maybe. It all depends on who's playing. If it's not someone interesting then I might just stay in and try to write some of my own music."

Another lie. All she really wanted to do was catch up on sleep and maybe watch some new show about a cult in Texas.

Ben deflated and took a sip of his coffee. "Gotchu. I vibe that. Speaking of music, did you hear about that new venue that opened up in West Hollywood? I heard they're looking for new artists to perform. Maybe you can kick off your tour there."

Stevie's eyes looked up from her mediocre latte, "Really? That's lit. The band has been looking for more potential venues to add to the tour if we end up doing one."

More lies. Her voice was scratchy and she felt burned out. She was in no way ready to go on stage anytime soon. No matter how much she loved it and how confident she was about the fact that the venue would excitedly have them perform a show there.

Ben nodded. "You should definitely check it out. I'm sure they'd love you guys."

Stevie felt a little bit of regret about how she'd been treating her music the last few months. She had been focusing so much on her day job and doing late-night hangouts with her friends that she had neglected her passion for music. She put that thought on a shelf like the ones about her mother and decided that maybe she'd focus on it more tomorrow.

ABOVE ALL THE LIGHTS

Stevie had just wanted to go home after her "awkward" work day, feeling drained and uninspired. Stevie trudged toward her Echo Park apartment building. The building looked a bit run-down, with chipped paint and missing screens on some of the windows with a faded mustard yellow color, a small parking lot on the side, and palm trees lining the busy street. Stevie dragged herself up the stairs to her second-floor apartment. She could hear the sound of traffic as she climbed the stairs. As she walked down the hallway to her unit, she noticed a few wilted plants in pots outside some of the other doors. The place was going to hell, but so was she. They were completely compatible. She finished her keys out of her pocket and unlocked the door to her unit, stepping inside with a sigh of relief.

It might've been small and sparsely furnished but it was home. For now at least. A futon couch and coffee table were the only pieces of furniture in the living area, which was all she could afford. She assumed that the walls inside her apartment were once white, but now they were musky with a tint of yellow that only made her think of the waiting room Stevie had to sit in as a kid when her mom visited her parole officer. The few scuff marks and chips in the paint that surrounded her now didn't bother her as much as that memory. Her mom, always invading her thoughts.

The hardwood floors of her unit creaked under her feet as she stepped in and dropped her bag on the couch and headed to the kitchen, if you could call it that. Everything was outdated but still worked. She had grown so accustomed to the sound of the fridge humming in the background that she actually found comfort in it. She grabbed a bottle of water from the fridge and let out a heavy sigh as she plopped down on her futon.

Her hangout with Ben made her feel unsteady with her life. She slumped onto her futon, staring blankly at the ceiling, trying to muster up the energy to write the music that she initially lied to Ben about.

She stared at her notebook for what seemed like decades. Everytime Stevie picked up her pen the only thing she could write was 'Pepsi' and then she'd scratch it out and then would write 'Coke'.

She threw her pen down and paced around the apartment, turning music on and off, occasionally fucking with the string on her American Apparel hoodie, trying to decide between 'Pepsi' and 'Coke'.

"This song is entirely fucked. What am I even trying to write?" Stevie thought. The only thing she knew was that she found it amusing to have 'Coke" mean cocaine and not soda. It would be both clever and edgy.

"And pathetic," she thought.

Stevie sat down and remembered being a teenager in her friend's garage playing music. She didn't care about whether her music was clever or not then. "It should be simple like that. Life should be simple like that," She thought.

Every little thing she felt at that moment was both petty and selfish. She felt like she was stuck in this life in perpetuity of anger, fear, anxiety, and dread.

She remembered her therapist said that there were only four primary emotions but a BuzzFeed article said there are eight. Only two of the emotions she was feeling at the moment existed on either list. The others she just didn't fully comprehend, so she decided not to dwell on it much longer. Stevie stared at the chipped paint on one of her walls that was just getting worse. She could always call her super but he gave her the creeps. His name was Wayne- a tiny, scruffy-looking man who always wore a stained white t-shirt that was several sizes too small and a pair of frayed jeans that were held up by suspenders and suspenders alone. If he didn't have such an unshaven face lined with deep wrinkles and greasy hair constantly slicked back in a messy ponytail, she'd say he gave her Boston Strangler vibes. A guy looking like that wouldn't likely be allowed past any door he knocked on without 24hrs notice and clear written approval. But that still didn't make her feel any better about being around him. Just because the guy looked way too awkward to be a serial killer didn't mean he wasn't one. Besides, anytime he came in, he brought a lingering smell of B.O. and tobacco that took days to air out.

So she decided to fix the issue herself by covering it up with a Cage The Elephant setlist she got when she went to a show of theirs with her ex-boyfriend. Stevie thought about him. His name was Alfie. An adorable name for an adorable guy who once said he was smitten with her, even after he found out she had cheated on him. To him, it didn't matter. He called her "lovey dovey girl" and accepted every weird thing that she brought to their relationship. He was a film editor who spent most of his days with her, watching movies and enamored with her raw talent and quirky personality.

She remembered playing Sims with him and building forts out of blankets and pillows at the apartment. Sometimes his roommate Isaac would bring his girlfriend Sammy over and they'd all hang out like that together. Isaac and Sammy drank Maker's Mark and Coors Light. Stevie and Alfie would typically drink soda. Sometimes a small beer or glass of wine if it fit a certain occasion. For the two of them, alcohol was a social thing. Something they'd drink on dates or at parties. Sometimes something light if they were on their own. But they never drank to get drunk. They both had moms who liked to drink a little too much so they stayed away from alcohol when they could. Or at least he did. She came over during a blackout one night during the summer to be with him because being alone in the dark is just sad.

He fell asleep on the mattress on the floor of his bedroom while his roommate, Isaac, was making Brass Monkeys in the tiny kitchenette of their ground-level apartment. Being a music lover, she had to try a Brass Monkey at least once. Beastie Boys were her childhood. Isaac was more than willing to not drink alone. They drank and talked about how his dad was once a steel magnate and how when he was cut off, he moved to Juarez for a short amount of time. Isaac went on and on about his adventures of being a drug mule while using terms like "jalopy" and "mocha-skinned girls" to the point that it drove Stevie bananas.

Halfway into his random babbling she got up and walked into Alfie's room. She moved his guitar and curled up next to him. When he woke up and smelled the alcohol on her breath, their relationship was over. Clearly, it was something that had slowly been building inside of him. Maybe her becoming more erratic and losing herself to music. Maybe it was her spending less time with him and he thought she was cheating on her. But at the end of the day, it was the alcohol that set him off. All of those behaviors, as normal as they were, struck too close to home for him. Which was something that should relate to only too much. It's strange the things that some people will tolerate and the things they couldn't.

She would know. Thanks to her mom she never really could get into the idea of twirling around with wine. Her mother would look glamorous one second and then fall down drunk the next. She typically would land on the couch or the carpet and pass out. But one time Stevie saw her mom going down in slow motion and knew she was going to hit the table by the TV instead. She was small but big enough to catch a 98 lbs alcoholic with problems balancing. While racing toward her mother, Stevie knocked over their Dorchester Portable Turntable. It was a grimy and wobbly excuse for a machine but it was her mother's reason for being. She said several times that it was her "spirit animal" and then would typically start trilling *Oh, spirit in the sky, what is love* or some other nonsensical lyrics until she'd fall asleep with a cigarette in her mouth. And Stevie broke it. Like she broke everything. Her promises, relationships, and maybe now even her band. She was her mother's daughter and she knew it was for that exact reason that Alfie left. He saw the writing on the wall in the same way that she saw the flaws on the one right in front of her.

Stevie again had to smack herself out of a memory of her childhood and then slapped the setlist on the wall carelessly. It didn't matter that the setlist was signed and worth at least $100. It didn't matter that she dented the wall in the process. She sat back down on her futon, grabbed her pen, and scribbled 'pepsi/coke' thinking that by joining them into one word, the song could be more interesting. Stevie wrote some more, sprinkling in some lines that were inspired by that relationship, and then scratched it all out. This idea was a hopeless attempt to appear cooler than she was. She grabbed her guitar instead and just strummed until her mind went blank.

Her brain wasn't in any place to write something that had any true meaning, so she grabbed her MacBook Air instead to watch Netflix. She scrolled through the countless titles and began to worry that she might just be lonely.

But then remembered a time when Stevie Nicks said, *"Most women would not be happy being me. People say, 'But you're alone.' But I don't feel alone. I feel very un-alone."*

Alone didn't mean lonely. She remembered her old therapist had a plaque on her door that said that. Stevie never really retained what the therapist said about her mental health, but she did retain those words.

And then as if the universe read her mind, her phone lit up with a message from Finn.

"Hey Stevie, wanna hit the road and deliver some burgers tonight?" Finn's message read.

Stevie sighed and looked around her apartment, cluttered with clothes on the floor and unwashed dishes. She didn't really feel like leaving, but then felt like this was life telling her that she needed to get out.

"Ugh, fine," she replied to Finn's message. "I'll meet you outside in 15 minutes."

Stevie dragged herself off the futon and stumbled to her closet, pulling on a wrinkled t-shirt and some jeans. She looked in the mirror and groaned at her messy hair and tired eyes. "This is not a good look," she muttered to herself.

As she walked down the street to meet Finn, she couldn't shake the feeling that she was just going through the motions. But at least she wasn't going through those motions alone that night.

He was bouncing with energy when she got to his Prius, already scanning the app, looking for orders. "Hey girl!" he grinned. "You ready to help me make some moolah?"

Ugh, that word. Why did he always have to say cringey things like that? Stevie managed a half-smile and got into Finn's car. Typically, they'd spend the next few hours delivering overpriced food from bougie restaurants to people in the hills while chatting about music or complaining about the traffic.

But it was dead that night. They drove to

Hollywood Hills and parked near Mulholland Drive in hopes that someone with some legit cash would order something but hours went by. As they waited, they gazed out at the stunning view of the city below, the lights sparkling like jewels in the dark.

"It's wild to think about how many people are just hanging around down there right now," Finn said, breaking the silence. "All living their own lives, doing their own thing."

Stevie nodded, her eyes still fixed on the view. She had always loved the Hollywood Hills, with their sweeping vistas and glamorous aura. It was easy to forget about her struggles and her worries when she was up there, looking out at the world from above. As they sat silently, waiting for an order to come in, they heard the distant sound of a party down below. The bass thumped through the crisp night air, and Stevie could just make out the sound of people laughing and shouting.

"Sounds like someone is having a lit party," Finn said, his eyes gleaming with mischief.

"We should crash it."

Stevie rolled her eyes, but couldn't help laughing. "Yeah, because that's exactly what we need right now. To get kicked out of some fancy Hollywood party."

Finn grinned. "Hey! You never know. We might meet someone who can finally make you famous."

Stevie shook her head and laughed, "Not in this lifetime."

They both sighed.

"Today is fucked," Finn said as he leaned his head

against the car window.

Two minutes passed before Stevie said, "How about we just head out? We can drive really slow and stop by Swingers Diner for a bit. Maybe even grab a smoke outside for a bit?"

"Ok." Finn sighed while tussling his hair.

Fifteen minutes later Finn and Stevie were parked next to Swingers Diner and smoking Natural American Spirits.

"I'm tired of work. I love the store and my coworkers, but it feels like I'm just wasting time there and waiting for death or something."

Stevie passed the cigarette to Finn.

"This barely even is a job and it sucks too," Finn said as he took a quick drag.

"It seems like that's the point of jobs. To suck."

"Yeah. They suck. We've been sitting around for like five hours now and all I can think is, 'I'm going to be five hours closer to death when we're done tonight.' I mean, that's if we even stopped right now. I'm just considering this a break until something comes up. I still have my app open so for me the clock is still ticking."

"If you think about it, work seems pointless," Stevie said.

"If you think about anything, it starts to seem pointless," Finn said while tossing what was left of the cigarette into the street.

Before Stevie could say something he grinned, "What?! It's someone's job to clean these streets. If they aren't dirty, then those people won't have jobs.

I'm simply doing my civic responsibility"

They both burst out laughing and pulled out another smoke to share.

"So what were we saying before that? Oh yeah! Life is really depressing right now," Stevie said, handing Finn the American Spirit.

"I don't know. I think it's always been depressing but now we have Twitter and Instagram out there to help disseminate this 'Great Saddening' that we've always been feeling."

"You're right. It's just another thing now. I read an article on Apple News the other day that spoke about the 20th century being the thawing-out period of dejection and angst. A sudden surge of depression being seen as COOL. I think the article was about Woodstock '99 or something. But the 'Great Saddening' probably actually started way earlier than that. Like, forget Kurt Cobain. Think Dostoyevsky or that crazy motherfucker, Voltaire. He literally wrote that 'man was born to live either in misery or in boredom'. Hell, even centuries before that they had depressing Greek plays that are epic even to this day. But maybe the article was right. Maybe there was some form of existential shift in the late 20th century. It does seem like it's suddenly lit to have whatever weird emotion you can think of. Maybe it had to happen. Like mentally. Maybe we needed it to happen, to cope with the World Wars, or Atom Bomb, or the Holocaust, or Columbine, or some other form of mechanized terror that I can't even think of right now. I don't know. Why is this even something we're talking about? Let's just blame MTV and be done with it," Stevie said.

"Because it's COOL," Finn said.

Stevie laughed in a deflated way.

"I feel best when I'm listening to depressing music," she said.

"I like to watch depressing movies. Have you seen *Donnie Darko*?" Finn asked.

"Yeah. That's the one Jake Gyllenhall movie I actually like. That and maybe *Zodiac*." Stevie said.

"*Darko* definitely is Jake at his best." Finn took a hit, "But you can never go wrong with David Fincher."

He exhaled smoke all over her. She knew she'd have to wash all of her clothes when she got home. Stevie hated the way that the scent of tobacco lingered on your clothes and in your house and in your car and even in your hair. She never knew she wreaked of tobacco until she moved out of her mother's house. Ever since she was so keenly aware of it. It didn't stop her from smoking occasionally, but it did make her know to shower and clean her clothes immediately when she was done. And to never smoke anywhere she liked.

Stevie took one final drag before throwing the cigarette into the street. She exhaled a cloud of smoke into the cool night air and looked over at Finn, who was standing beside her.

"Civic duty. Right?"

"Right," Finn just smiled at her dorkiness.

"You ready to head in?" Finn asked her.

"Fuck yeah," she looked around, "this place is

dead anyway."

She couldn't stop laughing as Finn just nodded and started motioning her toward the entrance of the Swingers Diner.

Stevie could hear the faint sound of music drifting out from the street that was now at their back as they approached the diner. A neon sign somewhere above flickered, casting an eerie blue light over the sidewalk.

Finn pushed open the door, and they stepped inside. The air was thick with the scent of fried food and coffee. The diner was nice and empty for once.

Stevie scanned the room and spotted a booth in the corner. She motioned to Finn, and they made their way over to it. As they sat down, a waitress appeared at their table.

"Can I get you two anything to drink?" she asked.

"Milkshake," Stevie said, and Finn nodded in agreement.

The waitress quickly scratched their order onto the pad she was carrying and disappeared into the kitchen. Stevie leaned back in her seat and surveyed the retro diner. The walls were adorned with vintage movie posters, photos, and 50s memorabilia, giving the diner a sense of nostalgia. There was even a jukebox in the corner playing Buddy Holly music just in case people didn't realize that this was a retro diner.

Stevie felt a sense of belonging in this place. She couldn't believe that she lived in LA for so long and had never found this place. She and Finn could have been coming there for years and be regulars. Instead, she had to overhear two customers over at Vinyl Haven talking about it the other day to know it even existed.

As they waited for their milkshakes, Stevie picked up her phone. Finn gave her a disapproving look but didn't say anything. Stevie knew it was shitty and she should be more present, but it was the one addiction she had.

Their milkshakes finally arrived, and Stevie took a sip. It was thick and chocolaty, just the way she liked it. The two sat in silence, sipping their drinks and watching the world go by.

Stevie knew they couldn't stay here forever. A morning would soon come and they'd both have things to do and places to be.

As she finished her shake, Stevie stood up, "I wanna run to the bathroom real quick."

She casually went in and looked around to see if anyone else was in there before taking her phone back out to take a mirror selfie captioned: Just Another LA Night...

I LAID UP FOR
HOURS IN A DAZE

Stevie had a lot on her mind as she left the Swingers Diner with Finn. Despite the late hour, the streets of LA were still alive with activity. The neon signs and the cacophony of honking cars filled the air, making it hard for Stevie to focus on anything other than the surreal surroundings. Finn led the way back to the car, and Stevie followed, lost in thought.

As they drove home, Stevie couldn't help but think about the dream she had the night before. It was so vivid, so real. The feeling of panic she felt in the labyrinth was still fresh in her mind. And the way the Dreamscape moved with eyes that looked at her, cold and unfeeling, made her shiver.

She tried to shake off the feeling and focus on the present. Finn was talking, but Stevie was only half-listening. She was lost in thought, thinking about the dream, wondering what it meant. It had to mean something, right? Dreams don't just happen for no reason.

When they finally arrived at Stevie's apartment building, Finn said goodnight and disappeared into the night.

Stevie had barely been home for more than an hour when she felt a sudden wave of exhaustion wash over her. Despite feeling utterly spent, she knew that sleep wouldn't come easily tonight - not after the strange dreams she'd had the night before.

She closed her eyes and took a few deep breaths, trying to calm her racing thoughts. But no matter how hard she tried to clear her mind, she couldn't shake the feeling that something was off. Something was different about her dreams lately, and she couldn't quite put her finger on what it was.

Eventually, she drifted off into a zombie-like sleep. And as she slept, her vivid dreams came back.

This time, she found herself standing in a lush forest, surrounded by tall buildings that towered overhead that had been overtaken by vegetation. It was as if a switch flipped one day making all humans disappear from the planet, and this is what remained. The air was thick with the scent of pine, damp earth, and rusted metal. The ground she walked on swayed in the wind causing her to reclaim her balance every few minutes. Stevie looked around, feeling disoriented, and saw that she was yet again, alone.

But as she began to drift through the woods as if she were floating on air, she heard a faint rustling in the underbrush. She froze, her heart racing, and tried to peer out beyond the trees to see what was making the noise.

Suddenly, a figure emerged from the shadows. Not a "guardian" like last time. Here was a woman, chic and wearing all black, with long blondish hair that fell in loose waves around her shoulders. Her eyes glowed an eerie shade of green. It should've terrified her but instead, it just drew her in further.

Stevie gasped, feeling a sense of recognition wash over her. She knew this woman, somehow - knew her in a way that went deeper than words.

"Stevie," the woman said, her voice soft and lilting like flowers on a rainy day in Seattle. "It's good to see you again."

Stevie felt a shiver run down her spine. "Do I

know you?" she asked.

The woman smiled. "In a way," she said. "I am a part of you, Stevie. A part that you have been denying for too long."

Stevie felt a sudden surge of fear rise up in her throat. "What are you talking about?" she demanded. The words "Fight Or Flight" now rang loudly in her mind.

The woman stepped closer, her eyes fixed on Stevie's face. "You know what I mean," she said.

"You've been running too long. It's time to face the truth, Stevie. Time to embrace who we were born to be."

Stevie felt a sense of panic rise up inside her. She couldn't fully make out the words that the woman was saying to her, but she felt like these words had been spoken to her before.

The ethereal woman began to fade away, twirling like smoke blown into a whiskey glass. "Remember who you are, Stevie," she whispered, as she disappeared completely.

Stevie woke up with a start, her heart pounding in her chest. She sat upright in her bed, feeling dazed and confused, and tried to make sense of what she'd just seen. She looked around her dark and messy bedroom, trying to shake off the remnants of the dreamscape. It had been so vivid, so real, that she almost felt like it had actually happened.

Taking a long deep breath, she tried to calm herself down and clear her head. She knew that dwelling on the dream would only make it worse, and she needed to try to get back to sleep. She closed her eyes and tried to relax, willing herself to drift off again.

But it was no use. Her mind was too active, too filled with the images and emotions of the dream. She tossed and turned in her bed, trying to find a comfortable position, but nothing worked. She threw off her covers thinking that maybe she was feeling too hot or something. But every time she closed her eyes, she saw the same scenes from the dream, and her heart started pounding again.

After what felt like hours of futile attempts at sleep, Stevie finally gave up. She got out of bed and walked over to her window, pulling back the curtains to look out at the streets below, and for a brief moment, she felt a sense of calm wash over her.

But then she remembered the dream again, and her anxiety came rushing back. She wondered if she was finally following in her mother's footsteps by losing her mind or whether there was something her subconscious was telling her to pay attention to. Or maybe it was just a meaningless jumble of images, a byproduct of too much stress and too little sleep.

With a sigh, Stevie turned away from the window and headed back to her bed. She knew she wasn't going to get any more sleep tonight...

Strange, you never knew

Stevie eventually passed out at some point in the late hours of the night. Or early hours of the morning. Who's to say? She found herself deep in yet another vivid dream but this time it was one she'd been having on repeat for years: being stuck back in high school even though she knew she wasn't supposed to be there. But it was as if she had been transported back in time. Her heart was pounding as she tried to make sense of the situation.

As she made her way through the halls, she saw familiar faces. There was the douche who sat next to her in Spanish, her once best friend who was in band, and even the bitchy English teacher she had in Sophomore year. Stevie tried to get out of the situation, telling everyone who would listen that she had already graduated, but they kept appearing in front of her, saying she couldn't possibly be done with school. She didn't finish one course she was supposed to. Stevie then got stuck in a fugue state. She thought she had her degree? But did she really? Her mind was warped so she just went through the paces in utter confusion.

Stevie couldn't shake off the feeling of being trapped and suffocated by the overwhelming sense of dread like she was stuck in a never-ending loop.

Just as she was about to break down, she heard the sound of a ringing incessantly. After a while she realized it wasn't the dream but her phone ringing. Groaning, she fumbled for it on her nightstand but eventually found it on the floor next to her mattress. Her boss called her 5 times to ask why she wasn't at work yet.

Panic set in as Stevie realized that she had overslept

and missed her shift at the Vinyl Haven. She quickly sprang out of bed, feeling embarrassed and ashamed. But as she scrambled to get her clothes on she noticed the time on her phone. The shift was way over and she was fucked. She couldn't imagine Jack being angry or firing her. But she knew that he'd let her know that he expected more from her or was let down. Maybe even suggest that she was better than that. It was those kinds of words that stung her the most. She could handle anger. But the idea of not living up to someone's opinion of her always hit her in the gut. Not a blow but a slow jab that lingered.

She lay back down, trying to calm herself down and think of a way to fix the situation. But as she closed her eyes, all she could see were the distorted images of the night before. Strange and unsettling, she couldn't help but notice that it was the first good time that she'd had in a very long time. She'd had so many wins in the last year though. Her band, Electric Stardust, put their music on Spotify and they were becoming well known. Or well known in Echo Park and other indie spots of LA, that is. They were booking gigs and her following on Twitter was exploding. She should've been happy with that but every time something good happened, the more stressed she got. The perpetual need for her to one-up whatever she'd done last gave her crippling anxiety. The more successful she was, the harder life became.

Eventually, Stevie got out of bed and tried to distract herself with some TV, but she couldn't concentrate on anything. Her mind was everywhere, from the dream to the "Great Saddening" to the fear of losing her job and all the way to her constant worrying about her band. She couldn't make sense of any of it. Stevie went to the espresso machine that her old roommate forgot when they moved out and attempted to make a better hazelnut latte than the one she had the day before with Ben. But like everything that day, it sucked. She drank it anyway and decided to go out on her fire escape in an attempt to slow down her thoughts. And they did. Hours went by and her coffee got cold and then suddenly there was a knock on her door.

Stevie groaned at the thought of having to leave the fire escape and decided to just poke her head inside and ask who was there. And randomly enough, it was Claire, coming to check on her after hearing she missed work.

A big, 'WHAT THE FUCK?' rang through Stevie's mind. Out of all the people from Vinyl Haven that could possibly want to check on her, Claire was the lowest on the list. Hell, she wasn't really on the list at all. She didn't dislike Claire but instead was rather indifferent towards her. They worked around each other more than worked with each other.

Strange.

"Hey, Stevie, are you okay?" Claire asked through the door. "I was worried when you didn't show up for your shift today."

Stevie considered explaining what happened but

felt embarrassed about even the idea of it.

She hesitated for a moment and then let Claire in.

"Hey, Claire," Stevie said with a sheepish smile as she opened the door. "Sorry about missing work. I overslept."

"Is everything okay?" Claire asked, stepping inside.

"I've been vacillating between good and downish. I was out pretty late last night and overslept. For some reason, I'm starting to feel down today. How are you doing?" Stevie asked Claire while leading her toward the fire escape that she had to abandon to open the door.

"I know that feeling," Claire awkwardly joined Stevie out there while evading the question.

"Sorry, I didn't message Jack earlier. Didn't mean to worry anyone. Just figured that since the shift was over that it didn't matter. I've been sitting out here generally reading tweets and not doing anything. Anytime I thought of leaving the apartment something amusing would happen out there on the streets, and I would just abandon thinking about it," Stevie shrugged as she took a long swig of coffee.

"Anything particularly amusing?" Claire finally asked, finally sitting down with her backpack beside her.

"A couple got into a very weird fight. No idea what it was about. But the wife was screaming at the husband that she didn't want to make a scene and he just got in their car and yelled out, 'A. SCENE. HAS. BEEN. MADE.' then drove off without her."

"Alright, people are just fucking being weird in general today," Claire laughed.

Stevie realized that this was the first time Claire had not only legitimately spoken with her but it was also the first time that she had seen Claire laugh. She felt a bit more at ease about talking to her in a "real" way.

"I felt very stuck in reality today. I'd like to feel more in my head so I could at least write or something, but I couldn't. So here I am," Stevie put her coffee down.

"You want coffee?" She asked Claire and got up to go to her shitty espresso machine.

"I've had no sleep, Adderall, and 2 cups of coffee today. I was bored at work I think. But why not?" Claire said, fully into talking to Stevie now.

"I made bad coffee and I'm still feeling kinda meh. You sure you don't want something else?" Stevie asked, "Maybe go out for a drink instead?"

Claire randomly started rummaging through her backpack making Stevie wonder if she had a flask in there or something.

"I almost forgot! I brought you something. Noticed how into *Rumours* you were yesterday. Wasn't sure if you'd heard *Tusk* or not," Claire said, happily pulling out that album that Stevie had been forced to listen to at least 11 times.

She liked some of the songs but always felt like it had the shittiest cover. What was the deal with the dog? It lacked the mystical nature that made the band worth listening to.

"Oh whoa! Thanks," Stevie faked excitement as if she'd never even heard of it.

"Wanna listen to it for a bit and then head out?"

"Yeah, it's too early for going out to a bar anyways. Throw it on and we can listen from out here with the coffee," Claire said.

Stevie hesitantly put it on loud enough for them to hear from the fire escape and made the coffee that she initially offered Claire. Instead of the Rwanda Kanzue roast from Alana's that she was originally going to make, she pivoted to their Sugar H20 Decaf blend. Claire was clearly already amped up enough.

While making the coffee, she could sort of hear Claire saying something about poetry. Stevie couldn't decide if this was directed toward her or if Claire's mood was so elevated that she was just talking aloud. Stevie handed Claire the coffee and a glass of water in hopes that she'd favor the water. She fumbled about for a bit and then finally asked about the poetry thing.

"Sorry, I turned the music loud and I couldn't hear much while I was making the coffee. Did you say something about poetry?"

"Oh yeah, it's nothing I guess. Was just loving it out here and thinking that this is a perfect spot to write from. Is this where you come to write your music?"

"Sometimes, when my brain allows me at least," Stevie laughed. "You write poetry I'm guessing?"

"Sometimes...when my brain allows it," Claire said while taking a sip of coffee.

Water: Rejected.

"Life has felt instantly and profoundly bleak and empty for me. But in the storage room yesterday my brain was like, *I have to write*. I just started jotting stuff out on my notes app but then people started coming into the store and stuff, so I was ultimately destroyed in my attempt to finish any of the poems I started. I liked where I was going with them I think," Claire ranted on until a car alarm broke her train of thought.

The sun was slowly setting as the two finished the coffee.

"Can I check out any of your poems?" Stevie asked and immediately regretted. As a musician, she knew how vulnerable one could feel during the early stages of writing something.

"Maybe after we've had a few drinks," Claire winced, "where did you wanna go anyways?"

"I was thinking Cha Cha Lounge in Silver Lake," Stevie put her jacket on.

Claire grabbed hers too, "Lit. Let's head out."

Stevie and Claire stepped out of her apartment building in Echo Park, ready to head out for a drink. Claire was feeling lit and Stevie was eager to get out of her apartment in hopes that she could get Claire to zen out after the reveal of her having so much coffee and Adderall. She didn't take a sip of water while on the fire escape and Stevie's only wish was that alcohol would bring Claire down a notch or two. She didn't have much experience with shit like that. She even had less experience with getting someone successfully out of her apartment without the song and dance of yawning and checking the time and signaling to them that it's time to leave and then trying to usher them out her door. She was California born and bred, but she was told that this procedure that she seemed to always go through was called a "Midwestern Goodbye". It surely was something that she might've picked on her dad's side. So many holidays she had to spend going to Milwaukee to see a side of the family she didn't know, only to have to gossip to her drunk mom about how awful they were when she got home. God forbid she say anything good about them, her mother would've lost it. Divorce is hard. Growing up alone with an erratic mother was even harder. But such is life.

As Claire and Stevie waited for their Uber to arrive, they chatted about the bar they were headed to, the Cha Cha Lounge in Silver Lake. Stevie's head already hurt but she was determined to act as excited as possible. This "Claire experience" was new and she wasn't about to push away people at this point in her life. Besides, she was so whimsically macabre that it made Stevie think she found another member of her tribe. She read once, that eons ago, that there were nomadic tribes that wandered the Earth, and within each of these tribes were enchanted beings. Stevie often considered herself one such being. But like all things, these tribes dissipated with time. Scattered across the seas and continents, hopelessly in search of some deeper meaning. But every now and again, one being like herself might come across another enchanted being. Every now and again, that being is a lost member of their *tribe*. Stevie felt that Claire could be one such being. How these tribes manifested, she couldn't say.

Stevie liked to imagine that these tribes were always destined to come back and find each other. It was just a matter of time. She imagined them not just as tribal nomads but as beings that were fundamentally connected in a way that went beyond consciousness. An idea that these beings are perpetually drawn to each other because they are simply made up of star stuff. Stevie imagined atoms being near each other when the universe began and over time, the same atoms would keep coming back together creating a bond that was beyond reason. A spiritual tribe that went all the way back to the beginning of time itself. Enchanted beings made of star stuff, wandering alone until they eventually would find those atoms that they were once close to. A tribe that didn't walk the Earth together out of necessity but one that was always meant to be.

Stevie's thoughts slowly faded like a cool mist in some John Carpenter movie. Reality drew her back to the present.

"I've heard they have the best margaritas in town," Claire said with a grin.

Stevie nodded in weary agreement. "Yeah, I can't wait to try one."

Just then, a sleek black car pulled up to the curb. The driver rolled down the window and greeted them with a smile.

"Stevie?" he asked.

"That's us, are you Carlos?" Stevie asked, and they climbed into the backseat as he confirmed. She always asked because she didn't know shit about cars. The app said it was a black car. This was a black car. But you can never be too careful. Finn told her about so many fucked up Uber experiences he had and he was a driver.

As the car pulled away from the curb, Stevie and Claire settled back into their seats and started chatting more about what they left off with at the fire escape. Stevie was a tortured musician with no self-esteem. Claire was a tortured poet with no self-esteem. It was a pity they never spoke about this shit earlier. They could've possibly become friends when Stevie first started working at Vinyl Haven instead of two years in. The driver, a weird but friendly guy, chimed in every once in a while with a comment or a joke. He clearly was aiming for a good rating and tip. As an introvert, Stevie wished there was something on these apps that allowed you the option to decide whether you wanted the driver to do small talk or just leave you be in silence. She would wear AirPods often, hoping they'd get the message that she didn't want to talk but most of the time they just didn't care or just didn't notice maybe because of her long hair. Either way, it was killing the mood for him to insert himself into their conversation every few minutes.

Luckily, the ride to the Cha Cha Lounge wasn't long, but it was long enough to give them a chance to take in the sights of a lifestyle neither could ever afford. They passed by trendy coffee shops, vintage clothing stores, and hipster bars. Stevie and Claire couldn't help but feel a little bit envious of the people they saw walking down the street, all looking effortlessly cool and stylish.

Finally, the car pulled up in front of the Cha Cha Lounge. Stevie and Claire thanked Carlos and stepped out of the car.

They looked up at the eye-catching and colorful building that would be hard to miss by someone even a block away. A single-story structure with a flat roof, painted in bright shades of pink, yellow, and green. The walls are adorned with colorful murals and street art, giving it a bohemian and eclectic feel.

The entrance even featured yet another neon sign that said Cha Cha Lounge and had a small outdoor patio area fenced in with plants and hanging lights, only adding to the very hipster ambiance. Stevie wondered for a second whether they should hang outside or inside but felt a draft and knew she'd get cold in only a t-shirt and American Apparel hoodie.

Stevie and Claire stepped into the crowded lounge, the lively hum of conversation and music hitting them like a wall. The air was thick with the smell of alcohol and the warmth of bodies pressed together in the cramped space. They scanned the room, looking for an open table or booth, but to no avail.

"There's no way we're going to find a seat in here," Claire said, her voice barely audible over the din of the crowd.

Stevie nodded in agreement, feeling a little disappointed. She had been hoping to sit down and relax for a bit but as she looked around at the packed room, she realized that they would have to make do.

"Looks like we're going to have to saddle up to the bar," she said, a hint of resignation in her voice.

Claire grimaced, but there was no other choice. They pushed their way through the crowd, dodging people left and right, until they finally made it to the bar in the center of the room. Even with its long, curved shape that was meant to make the space more open, the only seats available were two stools at the far end, next to a group of rowdy guys shouting over each other.

"Great," Claire muttered as they squeezed onto the stools. "This is going to be fun."

Stevie sensed Claire's desperation to be optimistic. "At least we're getting the full vibe of the place," she said, gesturing up towards hanging lights overhead and then pointing out the wide variety of vintage posters and such.

It was as if they stumbled into a dimly lit bar in Tijuana. Or at least what a rich white person might think a dimly lit bar in Tijuana would look like. Immediately this brought her back to the late-night conversations she had with Isaac when she was at Alfie's. She let her mind drift, wondering if he was full of shit or if he legit could say whether this place lived up to the vibe.

But as they ordered their drinks and tried to make conversation over the noise, Stevie was brought back down to reality and couldn't help but feel a little claustrophobic. The bar was so packed that she could barely move her arms without knocking into someone. And the guys next to them were getting louder and rowdier by the minute, making it hard to hear herself think.

Still, she was determined not to let it ruin the night. She turned to Claire and grinned.

"We may not have a table, but we've got drinks. That's all we need, right?"

Claire smiled back, looking a little relieved. "You're right. Let's just take in the vibe and have fun."

Stevie and Claire sat at the bar, nursing their margaritas and gossiping about their Vinyl Haven. As they talked, the energy of the crowded bar began to fade away, and they were lost in their own world of conversation.

But after an hour or so, Claire suddenly stood up and waved to the bartender. "Two shots of tequila, please!" she called out.

Stevie looked at her in surprise. "Tequila? I don't know if I'm ready for that."

Claire grinned. "Come on, Stevie. Live a little. Besides, I think I need something a little stronger before I share any of the terrible poems I told you about at your place. You know, when we were on the fire escape and you asked if you could check out the half-finished poems I was saying I did in the storeroom?"

Stevie hesitated for a moment, but then she nodded. "Okay, you're right. Let's do it. I know I need a few drinks before I can share songs of mine that are still in progress."

"Fuck yeah!" Claire slammed her hand on the bar in a way that sounded like it hurt.

The bartender placed two small glasses in front of them and poured the clear liquid into each one. Stevie raised her glass and looked at Claire. "To humiliating ourselves in pretentious and indulgent ways," she said, before downing the shot in one gulp.

Claire followed suit, feeling the warmth of the alcohol as it spread through her body.

"Wow," she said, laughing. "That's strong."

Stevie grinned, feeling the same burning sensation go down her throat. "It was your idea."

She hoped if she did enough shots it would give her that throaty, gruff, whiskey voice that amplified her songs. If Claire was gathering the courage to share some poems, Stevie was going to have to be ready to sing at least one song.

As they continued to drink and talk, Stevie and Claire found themselves opening up about all the fucked up little things that made them who they were. They laughed and hit on the bartender. Claire even opened up about how she just left her boyfriend. A famous poet. She wouldn't say who. But Stevie did know that it was a bicoastal relationship and he was a trust funder. Claire and her famous poet got their MFAs at NYU but moved to LA once they both got their degrees. Apparently, for a few years, things were okay. They both had "day jobs" and had published poetry collections. But his most recent one caught the attention of a celebrity who must not be named. They posted a picture of themselves with the book by a pool, and his fame skyrocketed. Got an agent, an actual book deal, and a small place in New York for him to stay while he finished writing his newest work. Unshockingly, he also got a girlfriend there who was nonexistent on social media, so Claire was unaware of her existence. Until two weeks ago that is, when Claire was FaceTiming him and the "nonexistent" East Coast girlfriend casually walked behind him on screen.

Claire couldn't decide what was worse: the fact that she helped him write some of the poems in his newest work or that the East Coast girlfriend was wearing her NYU sweater in the background. It all sucked.

By the time they finished their third shot, Stevie felt like she finally should ask Claire to recite to her at least one poem. Hopefully, it would take her mind off of the cheating, unnamed famous boyfriend. Stevie was prepared to fake enthusiasm if it sucked. She wasn't sure what to do if the poem was about the douchebag and made Claire more depressed. Either way, it was a risk she was willing to take to get them off of the "sad boi" kind of talk that they were drifting into. But before Stevie could say anything, Claire had turned to her and asked, "So what's your deal?"

"Deal?" Stevie repeated in a quizzical way, picking up another shot. "What the hell does that even mean?"

"Your DEAL," Claire said more emphatically. "Why don't you have a boyfriend? I've been on your Twitter. You don't mention a guy or have pictures of one anywhere. Is it a band thing where you keep shit professional or something? I'm not getting same-sex vibes from you. Not that I'd judge. But are you seeing someone? You sing about love sometimes."

This threw Stevie completely off guard. She was prepared to fake enthusiasm. Prepared to sing. Prepared to maybe even collab with Claire a bit. But she wasn't prepared to go deep into her own personal life. Listening to Claire's was hard enough. The whole question left Stevie frozen, introspectively trying to figure out how to actually answer that question. Lie? Say Claire was right and that she didn't share personal parts of her life on social media. Tell the truth? But ONLY admit to the part about being single? Or just let all the feelings come out and talk about how she lost the only person she thought she loved? Another member of her tribe.

She was like a water balloon. All her emotions were packed in there and Claire had just pricked it with a pin, unprepared for the deluge of emotion that was about to come.

Stevie's eyes did their best not to tear up, "I don't wanna talk about it. His name was Alfie. It's over. That's all there really is to it. You're right though. Like everything, I processed it by writing a song. Not one that will ever be heard under a stage light or via Spotify. Just a song that I needed to write. I needed it to be over."

"What did you need to be over, homie?"

Stevie knew that voice. She lifted her head up and saw Finn with a bag full of what looked like burritos.

"Did you just call me homie?" Stevie laughed at him. Relieved that suddenly the attention was on him and not her.

"It seemed nicer than: Tiny Human," he laughed while looking at his phone.

"Are you Dashing?"

"Nope. Just standing here for the fuck of it with

someone else's food that I couldn't afford if I wanted to," Finn smirked. He stood there awkwardly looking at Claire and Stevie noticed that Claire was smirking awkwardly at Finn.

"Aww fuck, sorry. Claire, this is Finn. Finn, this is Claire," she was gesturing back and forth to both of them, "Claire's from the record store. Finn *was* a DoorDasher before he got kicked off the app for not delivering food from Cha Cha Lounge to whatever rich asshole who ordered it."

She laughed at him.

"Cute," Finn scoffed with a smile on his face until he noticed the time on his phone.

"FUCK," he was scrambling his things together. "I'm gonna hurry out and drop this off. Before I get kicked off the app," he mocked Stevie.

"You two gonna be here for a bit?" He asked as the two laughed at him struggling to get everything together.

"Yeah, big guy. We'll be here," Stevie shooed him out.

"Lit! Okay, uhhh don't go anywhere. I'll be back in like 15," he shouted while running to his car.

"Gotchu," Stevie leaned back over toward Claire and raised yet another shot glass to Finn.

He rushed out of the Cha Cha Lounge to his car. He was clearly excited to see them but Stevie had the distinct impression he wasn't hyped by her as much as he was for Claire. She was, after all, a tall, leggy, brunette with pale blue eyes. One couldn't help but hear the song, *Pale Blue Eyes* by The Velvet Underground every time one looked at her. Fuck, if Stevie swung that way, she'd go for it. What she couldn't get was Claire's intrigue about Finn. He was what some people might call a "short king." He was fumbly, neurotic, with blonde messy hair and a wardrobe that made you think he lived through the "Grunge Rock" days. If he wasn't wearing flannel, he was wearing a cardigan one size too big for him with torn blue jeans.

"How do you know him?" Claire giggled at Stevie, not even trying to hide her attraction towards her DoorDashing friend.

"Not gonna lie, we legit both don't know exactly how we met but we've known each other for years. He doesn't move within our world though. But he's insanely supportive of me. Every time I get nervous about going on stage for a gig, I always spot him somewhere either in the back of the venue at the bar or near in front on the left-hand side of the stage. Told me if I ever begin to sweat it out that I can act like I'm just singing to him. I would never be nervous to do that because I know he legitimately doesn't care. Just wanted to be there. Humiliatingly once though, he brought a poster that said, "I heart the gypsy that you are," Stevie placed her hand on her forehead and slinked slightly down. The experience was both extremely cringe but funny.

She could notice Claire's disappointment and immediately realized that she had to clarify that Finn wasn't a love interest for her at all. Their relationship was purely platonic with a capital P. Not as close as a brother but closer than just a friend. Perhaps just another member of her tribe.

Claire smiled and just said, "Gotchu," while doing another shot.

Almost immediately Finn was back in the cozy atmospheric lounge, hanging by the pinball machine.

"Aight, I'm done for the night. I'd ask if you two wanted to have a drink with me but it looks like you're both at your Dorothy Parker stage of the night. Wanna work some of that out of your system with pinball and water? And by water, I mean dear fuck, hydrate."

Claire started slurring some random quote from the movie, *Waterboy*, making Stevie realize that Finn definitely had the right idea. She personally hated pinball. Or was at least indifferent toward it. But sometimes you just have to do things you don't want to.

That's what her mother consistently told her while she was growing up while forcing her to learn how to play guitar. Stevie loved it but she hated being told she had to do it. Something about not being able to choose to do something yourself made it less fun.

She closed out her tab and led Claire to Finn like she was handing her off to a lifeboat. They went past the retro signage, tropical plants, and more confident people dancing to whatever the hell the DJ was playing. Finn took the glasses of water that Stevie brought over and Claire's hand. They played for what felt like hours and Stevie watched, missing the times when she did things like that with Alfie. Here she was with her tribe and someone wasn't there. Several were in fact missing. She considered calling the band to play but knew if she did, they'd just pester her about wanting to tour. Dustin, Julie, and the others would have to wait another day.

She decided to happily play the third wheel instead. Or maybe she was being more like a Yente. Their laughter and the clanking of metal balls coming from the machine next to her, slowly became louder than the music that was making the ground vibrate.

She couldn't exactly tell if they were more into the game or each other. Either way, as their eyes darted back and forth across the machine, tracking the ball's movement. They were both trash-talking and joking with each other, clearly enjoying themselves.

Stevie was transfixed by their movements. The way they controlled the flippers, timing their shots just right to keep the ball in play, was mesmerizing. She could see the anticipation in both of their bodies, the laser-like focus in their eyes, as they struggled to keep score.

As she watched, she started to feel like she was part of the game herself, as if she was playing alongside the couple. Stevie could feel the tension in her own body, the excitement building as the ball ricocheted off the bumpers and barriers on the machine. Stevie found herself cheering them on silently as if her encouragement would somehow help them become happier people at the exact time and place.

The couple continued to play, and Stevie continued to watch. She noticed that they were both getting better at playing and keeping score. Each one learning from the other's "moves" and body language.

They were both making clever shots and racking up points, and the game became more intense as the score gap between them closed.

In the end, it was Claire who emerged victorious, with a final score that left Finn shaking his head in disbelief. Stevie watched as the couple high-fived each other, laughing and chatting about the game they had just played. As they walked toward Stevie she couldn't decide whether Claire was better at the game or if Finn threw it. Or maybe it was the trash-talking. But it didn't matter. Finn yanked Stevie toward the two of them causing her to spill her water.

"Come on, Jeffrey Dahmer. Let's take some pics in the photo booth. Goofy pics only!" He proclaimed loud enough for anyone within 60 feet of them could hear.

Claire looked confused about the Jeffrey Dahmer comment. Stevie could've explained it, but why spoil a whimsical night with an odd inside joke that she shared with Finn ever since the release of that miniseries starring Evan Peters? She wore the exact same style glasses as the infamous serial killer, enjoyed PBR, and could be painfully socially awkward at times. To add to all that, her father who abandoned her and her mother lived in Milwaukee. He had a thick accent that Stevie liked to mock when she'd come home from holidays that she spent there and joked about the fact that he too, worked at a chocolate factory. It was all too amusing to her and Finn. Claire could be macabre but Stevie wasn't sure just how dark and twisty she was. Only more time would tell.

Claire jumped at the idea of photobooth action and Stevie shook her head blithely while heading into the booth with the other two.

The photo booth was one of those classic ones, with a red curtain for a backdrop and a stool to sit on. As they sat down, Finn hit the button to start the countdown, and they began to strike some dorky poses.

For the first photo, they all stuck their tongues out and crossed their eyes. As the camera flashed, they burst out laughing, excited to see how it would turn out. For the next photo, they all flexed and tried to look tough, but ended up looking more like they were trying to hold in a sneeze.

As they took more photos, they got more creative with their poses. Claire put her hand on her head and pretended to faint, while Stevie stood behind her, pretending to catch her. Finn hopped out of the booth so he could stick his head through the curtain and make a funny face, trying to look like spies.

As they took their final photo, they all leaned in close to each other happily. No dorky pose was needed. As the camera flashed, they erupted into fits of laughter.

As they stepped out, they eagerly looked at the photo strip, which had captured all of the new direction that this LA night was headed in. They high-fived each other, proud of their nerdy antics, and headed back to the bar to decide what to do next.

"You two just wanna get out of here," Finn asked.

"Hell yeah, this place is dead anyway," Stevie

snickered. Another joke that flew over Claire's head.

Finn smiled at Stevie for a hot second and said, "Okay, perhaps you both are beyond going anywhere else."

He could see that the two had consumed a bit more alcohol than they could handle. Casually, offered them a ride home, rather than risk them taking an Uber back to Stevie's apartment in Echo Park. He used to rideshare himself but felt like two drunk girls would fare better with someone who actually knew them.

Finn helped Stevie and Claire into his car, making sure they were comfortable and buckled in. He could tell that they were both grateful for his help, and he was glad to be there for them. He was no white night. Just a friend who could be counted on.

As they drove through the winding roads of Silver Lake, the trio chatted and laughed. *Sunglasses at Night,* by Corey Hart, blasted from the car's stereo while Stevie and Claire discussed their plans for the future. Soon to be a world-famous poet. A musician on the rise. Finn felt a sense of warmth and contentment wash over him, hearing the two map out lives that he knew he'd never live. But he was happy to be there with them in the *here* and *now.* And one day he would be the old friend of the stars. It didn't bother him even a little bit.

After a few minutes, they reached Stevie's place in Echo Park. Claire was drunk and Stevie didn't know her address so she accepted that she'd have a roommate for the night.

Finn helped them out of the car and walked them to their door, wanting to make sure they got safely inside before leaving. Little did he know, the Midwestern Goodbye was about to happen instead.

"Thanks for the ride, Finn," said Claire, giving him a warm hug. "You're the best."

She hung by the car a bit, silently looking at each other until Stevie slowly started leading them to the door of her building.

"Oh! No, no, no, no! We were gonna get artsy together tonight. Remember the fire escape, Stevie?" she said in a drunk but matter-of-fact way.

Stevie sighed, hoping that Claire had forgotten the reason they even went to Cha Cha Lounge.

Claire demanded, "Grab your guitar! I fed you my depressing morsel of love lost. It's your turn."

She looked at Finn to briefly let him know, "My douchebag boyfriend just cheated on me. I was thinking of swearing off men for a while, but not all guys are douchebags I guess."

Stevie looked at the awkwardness as she was heading up her shitty stairs to grab her guitar. If that was flirting, then flirting is weird as fuck and she wanted no part of it. Stevie never actually flirted. Guys just always happened to be around. She never thirst-trapped or swooned over the people she was with. She was herself and for some odd reason that worked. She definitely didn't think she was one of those girls who was all dark and mysterious but didn't know she was beautiful the whole time. Her life wasn't some '90s movie. She wore her glasses. She wore black. She wasn't sure if she was mysterious. But she did know she was pretty. Not in that obvious kind of way. More in that indie movie kind of way. She continued up the stairs to get her guitar. The mating ritual outside was just too cringe.

Mirror in the Sky

Once Stevie got into her chaotic apartment she began searching for one of her guitars. She loved how Claire shouted at her in a way that made it sound like an actual musician only had one instrument. But it didn't matter. She lost her train of thought for a moment when she saw the Fleetwood Mac album still on her record table, half-drunk coffee on her fire escape, and clothes everywhere. Stevie scooped up a black cardigan, white t-shirt, and a beanie that said "Coffee Girl" that she got from the one time that her band played a gig in Portland. She loved coffee and *The Goonies* so the idea of taking a side trip after the show to Astoria was a no-brainer. Her whole band, Electric Stardust, came too. They were tribe. And when you find your tribe you stick together. Like *The Goonies*: Goonies never say die! They drove the 3 hours there just to see the house where it was filmed, see sea lions from the coves, and drink coffee on the docks where Dustin did the truffle shuffle while the rest of them thought up new songs. Before the day was up she got a hat from the coffee shop called, Coffee Girl, because she had no idea that Oregon was capable of being that cold. Both girls in the band got one. They jokingly said that the guys should too so they could all play their next show while wearing them, but it was to no avail. The dudes: Dustin, Tony, and Tyler outvoted The Girls: Julie and Stevie. The girls got their hats and then they went to watch *Ghostbusters* at some old theater instead.

The mere sight of the cap in her apartment made her long for them and experiences like that again. She put it snuggly on her head, grabbed her mandolin, and headed back down her shitty stairs to play the encore that her audience of two demanded. No matter how weird and awkward the idea sounded.

Stevie came out to find Finn on the curb, already listening to Claire performing some of her poetry to him while he smiled, amused at how theatrical she was about it. It wasn't slam poetry for sure. But the way she got so hyped and emphatically said each word made both Stevie and Finn feel like they were at a show. It was like punk rock met poetry. It was bizarre and exhilarating in a way that felt more right than any form of performance art she'd seen before. Claire was so wrong when she was talking about poetry at the bar. Asking friends to see this kind of poetry wasn't shitty at all.

She found her way around Claire and onto the curb to listen to the words that she was promised to hear. Claire immediately stopped and recognized Stevie's presence.

"My, babes! Alright, I'm gonna start over. That chill Finn?" Claire gestured to him.

He just smiled and nodded "Yes."

She jumped up and down a bit like a pogo stick and took in a deep breath. Looked at her phone and shouted:

Need to have this feeling

In the sun
You in my arms
A cloud overhead
It morphs into a dinosaur
And asks how tomorrow is gonna be

Stevie waited for a bit while Claire stopped and looked at her. Finn leaned over and whispered with a smile to Stevie, "That's it. It's done."

"Oh damn! That's really good, girl. Is that one of the ones you were doing while working yesterday?" Stevie immediately got as hyped as she was capable of being at the moment. She wanted Claire to know right then that poets were not the shittiest artists. There are shitty poets. But Claire wasn't one of them.

"Yes, ma'am," Claire nodded and smiled proudly. "I don't now if it should be longer or if it's good as is."

Claire looked at the words she had written in a more introspective way.

"No, it really creates a feeling in such a succinct way. I vote that you keep it as it is," Stevie raised her hand.

Finn took a look at Stevie and raised his hand happily as well, "Seconded."

"Aww, you guys. Legit? Can I read another? It doesn't have a title because I was interrupted yesterday but I definitely think it's better," Claire started scrolling through her phone. "Okay, here it is."

Her audience of two sat silently on the curb full of anticipation.

Claire began:

after i die
my ghost will come back
and it will say 'all my poems suck at least i don't have
a body now i'm still bored'

and then my ghost will commit suicide
and i will be born again
because that is what happens when your ghost
commits suicide
i will think 'this sucks the ghost screwed me over'
and if she was there she might agree and apologize
but she's not there
because she killed herself with a dream
and then vanished into the dream
and the dream flew into a blackhole
and the blackhole devoured the universe over the
course of five hundred billion years
and then god said 'maybe i won't do that again

"Wow," Stevie sat stunned. "That was a whole other vibe. That's a poem. Like a legit poem. What inspired that one?"

"I don't know," Claire sat down on the curb next to them. "Things have been ok in life I guess. But I've been having mild religious-esque panics and serious doubts about my writing. My mind seems to have short-circuited. I have been so low in terms of motivation it is insane but then the other day it occurred to write from more of a realistic standpoint. The boring stuff. It seems like that doesn't sound realistic at all. But it's the closest I've gotten to truth while writing. They're my real, mundane, hopeless thoughts about my life."

"No, it isn't weird at all. I feel like that all the time. You're writing what's real to you. You can't 'simulate' a mood that isn't there. Being panicked about life, as fucked as it sounds, is what drives me a lot. Sometimes an intense energy hijacks my mind and I write something that I could have never found the words for until that moment. It somehow becomes a vehicle for the mood I was experiencing and as a bonus, I have a song," Stevie reassured Claire.

Claire leaned her head on Stevie.

"It's different for you though. People want to hear what a musician feels. Poets are the shittiest 'artists' or whatever. Painters get to be like 'Hey come to my art exhibition' or you music people get to say 'Hey listen to my band'. But poetry? I feel like it's an inconvenience to ask someone to read my stuff, let alone come to a bookstore or coffee shop to hear it," Claire lamented while slowly leaning back onto the grass to look at the stars.

Apparently, Stevie reassuring her about how awesome she was, didn't deter Claire from feeling like poets were, for some reason, a rung beneath other artists.

Finn joined her on the grass and watched the stars, " I feel you. Like everyone who thinks they're interesting, I've tried to write. Every time I did, I tore myself apart eventually ending up in some form of stasis and almost feeling mute or at least radically reduced in my ability to truly express my emotional state. I was never sure what I wanted it to end up being. I have a thing for dissolution. No peace or real point. When that finally occurred to me that I just don't have the reproductive organs to write about myself like that."

He gently but cautiously put his hand on her shoulder, "It's not shitty to share something that is truly real to an audience that very likely loves you."

Stevie was struck by this. Finn was so not a physical contact kinda guy and every time he talked about girls he made it seem like he was one guy who couldn't be held down. Here he was, being tender with Claire and thoughtful about her boundaries. Finn wasn't a dirtbag. But he typically wasn't so sweet.

"I just wish I was able to tap into that feeling more. To reenter the mood of it all like I did yesterday," Claire sighed. "One time I took two lorazepam to center myself while writing. Instead, I was freaking out thinking something would definitely go wrong. That attempt exhausted me. Yeah, I finished something that felt true. But I also felt very fully used after writing it. It's been damn near impossible for me to have an emotional configuration like that without medication ever since."

"I'm right there with you," Stevie finally joined them on the moist grass. "I tried to write the other night before I went Dashing with Finn but it was a disaster. Later when we were driving home and listening to music, something made me be like "fuck I'm gonna do an all-nighter and just write. But when I got home I fell asleep instead."

"Fuck, have either of you considered seeing therapists for these kinds of issues?" Finn sat back up on the curb.

"I did once but I hated it. Felt like going to an impromptu one-man play," Stevie sat back up with him.

"I just try and sort my own feelings out. Ex-boyfriend helped a bit, but clearly, that's not something I can turn to anymore," Claire finally refound her place onto the curb. "I'm torn between a very dad-like perspective on my writing which is like 'your writing is a waste of time, you are just being a self-absorbed baby' and another perspective that's like 'yeah, whatever, stuff sucks but poetry sucks less. I'd rather travel to random places and read poems and get drunk than not."

"Dude, life is just full of stuff that tries to coerce you into thinking that things are bigger and more meaningful than it really is. So many aspects of culture are just bullies trying to get you to give your life to some cause, be it a religion, or a desire to make money and get married, or have kids. They're inconsequential things that society declares are the norm and it gives people permission to feel like what they are doing matters more than what you're doing. It turns them into missionaries almost. They want to save you. Set you on the right track because they couldn't possibly fathom that being on our track makes us happy. I'd rather be the needle in the haystack. Not the haystack," Finn went on.

He ranted about it for at least 20 more minutes, making Stevie feel more and more like this truly was her tribe. Again, she wanted to call her band who she knew would dig the fuck out of this talk but she didn't want to talk about maybe going on a damn tour.

She was scared that if she didn't talk with them about the possibility of a tour, though, she'd lose those members of her tribe. They didn't get that a tour could break the tribe though too. They'd be just like the ancient nomads who dissipated with time and she'd be lost without them. The bigger they got, there would be more responsibilities, more pressure, and more demand for them to become mainstream. She'd seen it countless times. She called them third-album bands: they gain an audience with one album, they'd get everyone's attention with the second one, and they'd suddenly change who they were to become a radio-friendly band that had songs played in the background of car commercials or worse, on elevators.

Mainstream society could get to them and they'd feel the pressure to settle down. To fit the mold of who society wanted them to be even more. Married with 2.5 children and a car who only hung with other families. They'd go to barbeques with their kids and then gossip about how sad it was that their friend hadn't settled down yet.

Both of these fears tugged at her in a way that made her stomach twist. She never wanted to settle down. If she fell in love then she'd accept it. She'd reciprocate it. Like she did with Alfie. Maybe she'd even have kids. But Stevie always knew that she'd want to put her lifestyle and career first. For the first time, she realized that the idea of that wasn't something her mother put in her head. Her mother had the impossible expectation that her daughter would one day be famous. But her mother could've never predicted that her parenting style would turn Stevie off of the idea of having kids like she did. Stevie found family in her friends. Her tribe. As she grew, her tribe grew and it didn't feel like a Greek Tragedy that society made it out to be.

"I feel so anxious about our place in the world," Claire said completely out of nowhere.

Finn handed her a Natural American Spirit.

"Don't we all?" He said smugly while trying to light it for her like some guy out of the '50s.

"Hey, if we're gonna smoke, let's stay on the curb and parking lot as much as possible. I don't want any forest fires happening because of your dumbasses and it being traced back here. I don't know how they find where it begins, but they always do," Stevie said abruptly.

Finn managed to finally light it, " One: those fires never start here. Two: take a drag."

Claire was clearly still going through it.

"I think we're slipping into a darkness that we can't really turn back from. Everything seems like it can quickly deteriorate into nothing and I'm not sure how I feel about that. When I think about our fucked up country facing conflicts abroad, it makes me think about how fragile everything is. I hate how far our influence reaches. But I'm also scared about what that influence is doing to us too. Am I thinking on this too much over here right now?" Claire asked.

"YES," Stevie and Finn both said at the same time.

"Are you going through low-level mania or something? I'm bipolar so it's not something to be weird about or anything. You just seem very scattered today. Or is this all just stress?" Stevie asked Claire, passing the cigarette to her.

"Who the fuck knows? Probably just stress from

shitty relationships and shitty writing. I feel like my body and mind need a break from the daily grind," Claire said.

Finn took the American Spirit from her, "Well that's what this is. We aren't grinding. We're living."

Stevie could sense that Claire was feeling dismissed and decided that the best thing she could do was be on Claire's side a little bit.

"I mean it's not that you're wrong though," she assured Claire. "I tried turning on the news last week. Barely watched 30 minutes before getting worked up. My Apple Watch showed my BPM going over 100. This feeling of slipping into a darkness is a total mood. I have this vibe that I can't shake, that something big and almost prophetic will go down soon. An end times kind of thing that will change the very way we live," Stevie said.

"EXACTLY," Claire threw her hands up. "That. That's what I was trying to say. I don't know if it's stress, capitalism, or society in general that's dragging us down. But something IS dragging us down. Oh. My. God. Let's make an album together. We can be punk poets like Patti Smith."

Claire threw herself at Stevie, who barely caught her. The two giggled and Stevie just decided to fucking go with it. These were the nights that she used to love. Before actually trying to be professional.

Stevie held Claire while laughing, "Okay, well first I would need to break from the band. Fuck 'em. We'd do an introspective album based on our messed up, sad existence. We could call it, 'Ecce Homo' originally from the Gospel of Saint John, the Latin Vulgate, my personal favorite...." She bowed her head smiling. "The one where Pontius Pilate tears Christ off the cross, as Jesus cries out to God, 'My Lord, Why have you forsaken me?' and he then throws Jesus down amongst a crowd of faithful Hebrew followers, and snarls, 'Ecce Homo' or 'Behold the man'. Nietzsche used it as the title of his autobiography, so why not us? I could never tell if the dude was just being dorky in some late 19th-century way or if he legit thought of himself as a celestial savior brought down to save us all. The concept would be totally sacrilege but it's not like anyone in this generation would give a fuck. Such a scandalous and profane way to present ourselves. It would be such a dark and twisty title for an album that we would create that bears witness to ourselves. To the darkness that we're all slipping into. Or we could call ourselves Stillwater and see if anyone gets it..."

There was silence while Claire propped herself back up and stared at Stevie in utter confusion. Stevie assumed that an NYU grad would've been into all of that. Especially after all the post-modern thoughts she had drunkenly shared earlier. It made Stevie remember the days when she'd be smoking weed with her band in the garage and they just said shit that made them feel smart even though they probably didn't know what they were talking about.

Wrong crowd. Dustin would've been into it. Julie would've been into it. Fuck, even Ben from the store would've found it hilarious.

"That's why you two maniacs need to create

art," Finn put out the cigarette on the curb, clearly unphased by any of the words that came out of Stevie's mouth. In fact, he was rather used to it and barely paid attention as to whether Claire was keeping up with Stevie's maniacal thoughts once she got going.

He just stared off into space smoking, "Write poems, sing songs. Do whatever you two need to do to make this hellscape more bearable."

Stevie and Claire were quiet and Claire clearly wanted to change the vibe that she had started.

"Speaking of singing songs..." Claire desperately nudged Stevie who was now going through it herself. Stevie liked being open and free. Throwing all weird ideas out there with tribe. She immediately started doubting herself. She wondered if she wildly miscalculated what kind of person Claire was.

Claire picked up Stevie's mandolin and handed it to her, "Go on...if we're ever going to do a collaborative album as weird as that, I wanna see what you've got."

She desperately wanted to ease the tension and weirdness of everything. She wanted Stevie to open up and she had. The two had spent the night going back and forth trying to cover for each other's feelings. Up until now, it was mainly Stevie doing her best to keep her feel included.

Claire shook Stevie's shoulder gently, "Come on, I'd really like to hear what you were working on..."

Stevie sighed passively. Lost in introspection, she felt done with opening herself up to people. And sharing the music that she wrote without the intention of ever playing it professionally, might as well have been like cutting her heart out and handing it to them in hopes that they wouldn't crush it. Or worse, accidentally drop it.

"Ughhh. I would love to but it's been hard writing lately. I haven't had much downtime. My highs and lows have been crazy lately. Last year, I would sometimes write most of the day and sleep for only a few hours. Now I've been having shitty sleep, waking up at random times stressed about life and the future," Stevie shrugged, hoping that would get her out of it. Vulnerable enough for them to understand but not as vulnerable as sharing what she wrote.

"So is that why you're avoiding writing new songs?" Claire asked in a way that caught Stevie off guard. It felt genuine yet still off-putting. She couldn't decide if Claire was only tribe when she was drunk and erratic or if she was capable of it at all times. Her mind drifted back to Vinyl Haven. Days where Claire constantly badmouthed people's taste in music. She lowkey berated customers who didn't even know the right name of the albums they were looking for and once even refused to help a teenager wearing a fedora, who wanted to find the most recent Mumford & Sons album.

Stevie leaned back and freed herself from the situation, "I feel anytime I try to write, I just can't or like I'm just some over-indulgent asshole. That's why I really loved hearing your poems just now. You just put it out there. Kept it real."

Compliments tend to catch people off guard and she hoped it was enough to pivot the conversation back to Claire's poetry instead of her music.

"I dig your music though. It is real. Especially the last album. Like the songs sounded detached, almost indifferent to the immense sadness they dwelled in. You're talking to someone neurotic who has that incessant desire to write better. I get it. That's one of the most anxiety-inducing aspects, worrying about the flow and wording. I'd like to work more on that myself," Claire now seemed even more genuine while handing her the mandolin. Like she was truly trying to be apologetic for the weird mood that she had suddenly brought into their fun conversation just a bit ago.

She had been whimsically drunk but for some reason, Stevie's words sobered her up or something.

Tribe? Or not tribe? At that moment, who could say?

Claire pressed more, "I'm sure you've recently written at least something that keeps it real. You mentioned earlier that you were playing around with a song."

"Fine," Stevie picked up her tiny instrument that her friend, Birdman, gave her several years ago. Birdman's real name was Kai but his guitar straps always had birds on them. Stevie called him that once and sadly for Kai, it stuck. She always found the mandolin that he gave her more majestic than the acoustic guitar, which she was more known for playing. She didn't know why but she named it Caprica. The sound of the name fit the instrument and gave it an identity that the other things she played didn't. The only other instrument she tried to name was her electric guitar, Mobius. But it didn't stick. She could decide whether it was because she didn't play it enough or if it was due to the reason why she named it that. Why she picked that name, she'd never tell...

Stevie picked up Caprica and her notebook. She didn't want to fuck up a song she already felt embarrassed of. She had been thinking about Alfie so much that day that the words just poured out of her. She couldn't help it. But her audience was waiting. She looked at her sheet music and did her best to sing the words that she had scribbled down:

Fire in the Night

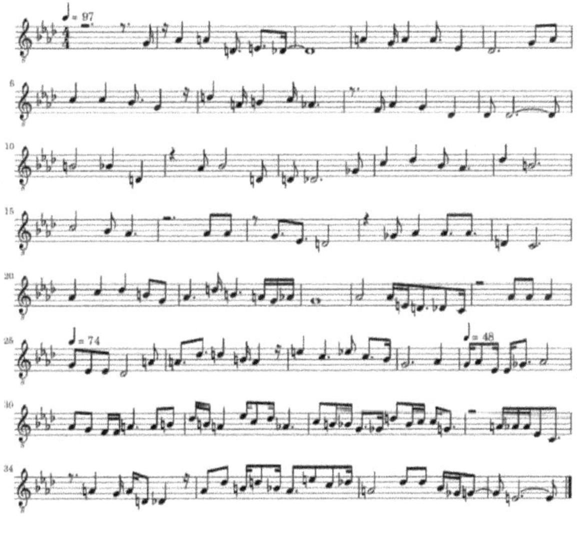

Verse 1:
I met him on a midsummer's day,
Let out a smile that couldn't go away,
Oh his eyes they sparkled, in the sun
I knew my soul had found it's one.

Chorus:
But here I'm lost in love again,
Can't get enough, my everlasting friend
Yes, my love, heart's desire,
Can't escape this burning fire.

Verse 2:
We danced beneath the moonlit sky,
His electric touch, made me feel alive,
Endless nights I spent with him,
A yearning lust to dive right in.

Chorus:

But here I'm lost in love again,
Can't, get enough, my everlasting friend
Yes, my love, heart's desire,
Can't escape this burning fire.

Bridge:

Oh, I never thought my soul would find,
Someone to make my spirit blind,
my love, I'm yours to forever keep,
Forever and always, in your arms I'll sleep.

Chorus:

But here, my heart's been lost again,
So many nights, you'd never comprehend
Stole my love, my desire, burning out
O-ohh I'm burning now

ANYONE WHO'S HAD A DREAM

Stevie had just said goodbye to Finn and set Claire up on the couch so she could crash for the night. She felt exhausted, both physically and mentally, as it had been a long week at work. She went to her room and changed into her Loser's Club t-shirt and torn pajama shorts before getting into bed. As she closed her eyes, she hoped to finally get a peaceful night's sleep.

But Stevie's subconscious had other plans. She found herself on a tour bus, surrounded by Electric Stardust, roadies, and groupies. The bus was cramped, and the smell of alcohol and cigarette smoke hung heavy in the air. Stevie didn't know where she was going or what she was doing, but she felt a sense of urgency like something important was about to happen.

As the tour bus drove on, Stevie caught glimpses of every city and concert venue she'd ever thought of. She heard the roar of the crowds and felt the adrenaline rush of being on stage. But as the dream went on, things took a weird turn. Clashes were happening between her band members about drugs and infidelity. Everything and everyone was falling apart. Overwhelming chaos and the pressure to perform began to make her heart race.

She suddenly found herself surrounded by strangers who were her new bandmates. As if her tribe could be replaced. They were headed to their next show, and Stevie couldn't shake off the feeling that even more things were about to go wrong. She didn't belong there, she didn't know the songs, and she didn't even know how to play an instrument.

Her anxiety only grew as she watched her

bandmates effortlessly play their instruments and interact with each other. No drugs. No infidelity. She felt like an outsider like she was intruding on their space. The bus grew smaller and more suffocating by the minute, and Stevie's heart raced faster and faster.

Suddenly, the bus screeched to a halt, and the new bandmates jumped out, leaving Stevie alone on the bus. Panic set in as she realized she didn't even know where they were, let alone how to find her way back home. She got off the bus and started wandering, hoping to find someone who could help her.

But instead of finding help, a van full of pissed-off fans who had been waiting for the band to arrive stopped at the shoulder of the road that she was on. They recognized her and immediately started yelling at her, blaming her for the band's absence. Stevie tried to explain that she didn't even know where they were and that those people weren't even the REAL Electric Stardust, but the fans wouldn't listen.

The situation only escalated from there, and Stevie found herself running away into a hazy suburban neighborhood. She darted behind trees and garages, trying to escape the angry fans who were hot on her heels. Eventually, she casually strolled into the backyard of a house party. The crowd was large enough that she thought she could just disappear into it. But just when she thought she had found a safe place to hide, the fans were there. At the party and looking for her. She climbed to the roof of the house but they grabbed her, ready to throw her off. Right as she was about to drop into what she thought was a pool, she woke up, gasping for air and drenched in sweat.

Stevie sat up in bed, trying to calm her racing heart. It had all been a dream, but it felt so vivid, so real. She took a few deep breaths, trying to shake off the feeling of panic that still lingered.

She lay there for a while, trying to calm down and make sense of what had just happened. It felt so real. She wondered if it was a sign that she should keep going in the music industry despite the pressure, or if it was her mind telling her to fade away and just live her life as she was living it now.

Eventually, Stevie fell back asleep, but the thoughts stayed with her. Over the next few days, she found herself thinking about them often, trying to decipher the meaning of them if there was any. She didn't talk to any of her friends about it but decided that she'd let her band know by the end of the week whether the tour was a go or not.

The secrets I do not know

The alarm on Stevie's iPhone went off at 10 in the morning. She groggily hit the snooze button and drifted back to sleep. When she finally woke up again, she was disoriented and confused. The room was bathed in golden afternoon light, and she could hear the distant sounds of traffic outside her window. She glanced at her phone and saw that it was already past 3 in the afternoon.

Feeling disappointed and frustrated, Stevie got out of bed and rubbed her eyes. She had wanted to make the most of her day off, but instead, she had slept through most of it. She checked to see if Claire was still on her couch but instead just found the blankets folded nicely on top of it and a note saying, "Thx, tiny human." She wondered if she was getting lazy or if she was losing her motivation in life. Stevie had always prided herself on her work ethic but lately, she had been struggling to find the same level of focus and drive that had propelled her to where she was today.

She walked over to the window and looked outside. The sun was still shining, but the day was already slipping away. She thought about calling some friends and seeing if they wanted to hang out, but she knew that most of them were probably busy with their own lives. She sighed and sat down on her bed, feeling a sense of ennui and frustration creeping over her. She pulled on the same clothes she wore the night before on the curb with the new members of her tribe, grabbed her "ROB" Ray-Ban sunglasses, and headed out into the late LA sunshine. She always liked the idea of meandering about Los Angeles at Golden Hour but never really had the chance due to her day job and night job. The chance to witness the warm and magical glow over the city was enough of a reason to go outside and get fresh air. The skyscrapers, palm trees, and sandy beaches would all be bathed in a soft, golden light that would turn pinkish. As the sun would begin to set over the Pacific Ocean. The light would filter through the city's smog and pollution, and create a hazy and dreamy atmosphere. The sky would transform into a palette of oranges, pinks, and purples, and provide a stunning backdrop for the city's iconic landmarks like the Hollywood sign, Griffith Observatory, and Santa Monica Pier.

Exaggerated shadows would create a dramatic contrast between the sky and the cityscape. And the beaches would take on a beautiful golden glow, with the sand and water reflecting the warm hues of the sunset.

It was something she could imagine writing a song about. But as she stepped out of her apartment she was met with the worn-out skies that hung over Echo Park. Today was not a day for fantasies.

As she wandered her neighborhood, Stevie couldn't help but feel a sense of loneliness. She had secretly hoped that one of her friends would call and invite her to do something, but her phone remained silent. She tried to push the feeling away, focusing instead on the way the light kind of played across the buildings. Not magical. But pleasant enough to take her mind off of her friends for one hot second. She stopped for a moment and looked up at the sky, wondering what she should do with her lost evening.

As she stood there, lost in thought, she noticed a bar across the street. It was an old-school joint named Monte Carlo Bar and had been around since the 1950s. It was the kind of place where the regulars knew each other's names, and the bartenders could make every drink they served like it was second nature. It was likely because it was a no-frills bar that didn't serve complicated cocktails. But who gives a fuck?

Stevie hesitated for a moment, wondering if she should go in. She wasn't sure if she was in the mood for a drink, but something about the place called out to her. She crossed the street and pushed open the door.

The bar was dimly lit and smelled of stale beer and cigarettes. A few patrons sat at the bar, nursing their drinks and chatting quietly. Stevie found a seat at the end of the bar and ordered a whiskey on the rocks.

As she sipped her drink, Stevie began to relax. The noise of the city outside seemed to fade away, and she felt as though she was in a bubble of calm. She took off her sunglasses and looked around the bar. She'd passed it so many times but never went in with the exception of that one dream she had a few nights back. It wasn't what she quite expected.

A dive: Yes.

But it felt more like a time hole in a wall. The bar felt like a fallen icon. A remnant from a time before gentrification that had somehow not yet been touched. It wasn't a crowded space but there were just enough bustling sounds that fit her vibe at the moment. She wanted to disappear into its very walls. Cease to exist for maybe like an hour or so. She'd never been to a place that looked more beaten down by life than her and she loved it. Disheveled artists, sketchy locals, and random people off the street could all feel at home here. Stevie was all three at the moment, making her Monte Carlo Bar's ideal clientele.

The only downside was the size and the presence of only one bartender who seemed like they wanted to talk. She shifted around on her red-topped barstool and put her sunglasses back on, trying to just sink into her drink as the bartender came back over to her.

"Hey, don't I know you?"

"Doubt it," she said while pretending to divert her attention elsewhere in hopes that he'd go to another unkempt artist.

"No, I do! You're that singer chick. The one from Electric Stardust. You're their lead singer. I love that new song you just came out with. What's it called again?" He asked himself while wiping down the bar with a cloth, firmly staying in that one spot.

"Oh yeah, *Whispers in the Wind*. That's the one. You write that one? Really made me think about how time moves in life. Sometimes too slow. Sometimes too fast," he pondered to himself, lost in thought.

Stevie slunked lower and then just simply answered, "Yeah, that was me."

"You people are gonna be big one day. My word to god," he put his cloth down and pulled out the tiny notebook that he sometimes took orders on. "Can I get you to sign this?"

Stevie was already ruffling through her pocket for some cash before he asked. She threw the money and the bar, getting up to leave, "Sorry man, I've got no pen. Millennials, right?"

She shrugged as if she gave a fuck and left.

This was not the place she wanted to be. Stevie needed to be nobody to everybody for at least one night.

THIS CITY DESERT MAKES

YOU FEEL SO ©OLD

Stevie stepped out of the bar, the sound of her nervous heart racing still ringing in her ears. She just needed a break. Now, she was outside, breathing in the cool night air, feeling a sense of relief as the noise of the bar slowly faded away. Stevie had always loved people-watching, and she decided to take a stroll through the streets of LA to clear her mind since drinking wasn't an option.

As she walked, Stevie took in the sights and sounds around her. She was buzzed and had no idea where she was after walking for almost an hour. The city was weirdly still alive, with people hustling to and fro. One guy she thinks was either trying to score smack or hire a hooker on the street across from her. The chick could play either part and she couldn't tell. For all she knew, the guy couldn't tell either. She saw couples walking hand in hand, groups of friends laughing and joking, and lone individuals lost in their own thoughts like herself.

A street performer drummed on a bucket beneath an overpass, his music filling the air with annoyance more than melody. Stevie was struck by the idea of making music out of anything, just to survive rather than to be famous. But then she saw a cop come up to him asking for a permit and the thought left her mind completely.

As she continued wandering aimlessly, Stevie noticed another homeless dude sitting on the sidewalk, holding a cardboard sign asking for help. She paused for a moment, contemplating whether to give him some money or not. She knew that it was just a temporary solution to a larger problem, but it was better than doing nothing. Hopefully, if enough people did this the city wouldn't smell like piss so much.

Further down the street, Stevie saw a gaggle of douche bros in a convertible with their stereo blaring Nickelback forcing everyone to suffer until they sped away. They were laughing and joking, carefree and wild.

Gotta love the patriarchy. If only she had the confidence of a mediocre white man, life might be a tad easier for her. She walked the streets with one hand in her pocket holding her iPhone and another holding her keys in case she needed a weapon. These douches had the luxury to live in the moment without a care in the world. To speed around, forcing people to listen to Nickelback while they acted like dicks. To annoy women about smack or sex. And to not have a cop approach them about any of it.

The more she walked, Stevie began to feel a sense of dread. Perhaps the whiskey had gotten to her more than she originally had thought. She felt a sense of disgust toward most of the people she saw on the streets, even the ones who seemed happy and well-meaning. They were all living their lives, navigating challenges and Stevie was stuck in one place. Her mind was stuck in a never ending cycle of apathy, depression, and longing. True, she had her people. She had her friends. She had her coworkers. She had her band that she'd been dodging calls from for days. But where the fuck were all of them now? Where were there people who she could be with and not have to be on brand or be nice to?

She slowly found herself passing what looked like a Deco-style hotel with a sign in the window that said it had a 24hr bar. She must've been downtown by the sight of things. The sign advertised $5 martinis. That was enough for her. She headed in.

I HAD TO STOP FOR THE NIGHT

Hotel Xavier was both ornate and imposing. On the outside, it seemed Deco but it might've had some Gothic details. Stevie was too buzzed to remember what she had learned about architecture back in humanities in her senior year of high school. All she knew was that the building was tall with a resplendent entrance, arched doorway, and rusty wrought-iron gates. It was the kind of place that could've been a landmark if it had any historical significance but from the looks of the lobby it didn't.

As Stevie entered the lobby, she was struck by the dark, moody atmosphere. It was the second dimly lit place she'd gone to that night, with walls painted in dark colors. You could tell the dust-ridden hotel had one time been a monument to splendor. However many decades ago? She couldn't tell. It did make her think of those old buildings she'd read about though. The ones that didn't have 13th floors so people wouldn't get anxious out of fear of the number 13. Stevie pondered what that phobia was named again but shrugged it off. She was actually particularly fond of the number due to the superstition. What people thought would happen on a 13th floor was beyond... *Triskaidekaphobia*! That's what it was called.

Stevie loved learning about the strange phobias people had. From the fear of magic to the fear of seeing a pattern of holes. People were fucked up and she loved it. They were called Rhabdophobia and Trypophobia by the way. Stevie especially remembered Rhabdophbia because her sophomore-year history teacher told the class about how he missed the days when teachers could actually physically punish their students. He insisted the word meant, 'fear of being beaten by a stick' and that always stuck with her. Stevie later found out that Rhabdophobia actually meant both.

But back to silly old-school superstitions...

Apparently, architects of these old as fuck, Deco-looking buildings would leave the number 13 off the blueprints and just have the floors go from 12 to 14. But it's not like they didn't have an empty inaccessible floor between the two. It was simply renamed. Having a 13th floor in the middle that you couldn't go to would be more amusing, but she understood the practicality of it all if you considered skipping the number 13 on an actual blueprint, practical that is.

As she lingered there for a bit, her mind drifted back to the feel of the lobby itself. It was a total mood.

It was musty but had a grand staircase made of mahogany, which led up to actual rooms she assumed. The staircase was flanked by large chandeliers, casting a warm, flickering glow over the otherwise darkened space.

She walked toward the check-in desk to ask where the bar actually was. It even had ornate carvings beneath the cobwebs that she accidentally swiped as she raised her hand to ring the bell to get some assistance. She overheard a groan and footsteps thumping in her direction from behind the desk so she decided to wait silently instead of ringing the bell again or just asking her question out loud. As she waited, she took in the opulent and refined feel of the space. All Stevie could think was that she really needed to get out of Echo Park more. LA had so many layers to it that she was still discovering each day.

She was met at the desk by the night manager named Don. He looked like he was 40 going on 60 and confused about which decade he was in, dressed in a tailored suit with flip flops and Buddy Holly-type glasses. He was curious, indeed. But far too weird to make any form of small talk with. Stevie simply wanted to go to the bar and drink their cheap alcohol. Since there seemed to be nothing else for Don to be doing at that time of night in the large and empty-looking hotel, he led her to the bar personally and then left her to it. She was surprised to see that the bar had a separate name from the hotel, but then again, Stevie wasn't sure if she'd ever actually gone to a bar in a hotel.

The bar she had just been led into was called "The Cecil Lounge." It was another dark and moody space, with a distinct vintage feel. But instead of making it seem chic, it gave off an atmosphere of decay and decadence. It was a long wooden bar, lined with stools and surrounded by shelves of liquor bottles from all eras. She imagined that if she asked the bartender, they might even have Absinth or Laudanum stashed away.

The lighting was low and intimate. The walls were decorated with vintage artwork and photos from what looked like the '30s.

There were several large circular booths with red velvet cushions in the center of the lounge, but only one person was hanging there.

The only other people in the room were the

bartender next to a mirrored wall, mixing drinks and chatting with a guest. And, the guest. Despite the desperate depiction of warmth in the space, it felt dark and desolate. Stevie was finally in the right place. The guy in the booth looked like an agent type and overheard the bartender call him Nick. She'd met quite a few throughout her musical career. And the guest at the bar was maybe her age, wearing a feather boa with a sequin top. Another possible hooker. But Stevie wasn't there to judge. Just drink. She grabbed a stool at the opposite end of the bar to show that she was in no need of company. Just alcohol.

She ordered a gin martini. The bartender, Webster, was a burly but well-dressed man with a mustache and forced smile. He poured Stevie's drink expertly and slid it across the bar to her.

"Thanks," Stevie said, taking a sip. "I don't think I've ever been to a place like here before."

The bartender nodded. "Yeah, a lot of people haven't but once you have it's hard to imagine a life without such a place. It has a way of staying with you. It's got a lot of history if you know what I mean."

Stevie smiled wistfully. As she sipped her drink, Stevie took in the sights and sounds of the bar. Music caught Stevie's attention. The young woman with the feather boa was now playing the piano in the corner, her fingers dancing over the keys as she sang a haunting ballad. Stevie recognized the song immediately, and she smiled as the still-possible hooker finished the last verse.

"Silver Springs," Stevie said, clapping her hands.

"Best flex in the history of music."

"Right?!" the still anonymous chick said. "What's your name?"

Stevie downed her $5 martini and told her the sad truth about her name and why she had it.

"At least your name means something to someone. Fuck, it means something to a lot of people. Mine is just Lily," she finally revealed.

Lily looked around to see if there was anyone else around other than Stevie, the dude in the booth, and the bartender. Seeing it was all clear, she made her way over to Stevie.

"I love music. I've been playing piano at the lounge here at night for years. Something about the trashy but vintage aesthetic appeals to me. It pays shit, and I mainly just get tips but the vibe is what I come for. It's better than any other job I've had," Lily took off her boa and took a small bump of coke that seemed to just manifest in front of them.

Lily gestured to Stevie, but Stevie just shook her head and politely declined.

"What's your day job?" Stevie asked, guessing it was something that the average person would want nothing to do with.

"I used to be a teacher," she smiled. "Or at least I went back to school to pursue a degree and credential in education. It just never really stuck; the pay and the stress. But during a summer off I went up to Northern California to help my friend at a medical marijuana co-op. I met a lot of interesting people, most of them were simple and easy enough to figure out - if you choose that life you can imagine most of the story behind it. - But the children were fascinating; not so much as individuals, but their perspectives and their understanding of the world... I guess these feral children demonstrated the effects of a factory-style education system."

"So to be clear, not a teacher then?" Stevie asked confused as fuck. She waved over Webster for another martini while waiting for her new "friend" Lily to explain.

" I mean, not EXACTLY. I guess in short, I studied education where I had to teach in order to complete the degree, spent a summer on a medical marijuana co-op, and feral children freak me out. Only interest I took away from all of it was the effects of factory-style education. Carl Jung wrote that we don't have ideas, ideas have us. Dostoyevsky toyed with this concept in his novel, "*The Possessed*."

Lily took one last bump and ordered a martini too. Stevie sat, processing it at all.

At least this wasn't an annoying cokehead, like the fan who tried to slip a gram into her hoodie after a gig once and refused to take it back. Or the New York artists who did it just to look cool. Lily was a whole other vibe and probably not a prostitute like Stevie originally assumed.

Stevie took another sip of her martini, "I feel like I haven't read enough Dostoyevsky in. I've only read *The Brothers Karamazov*. I like that concept though."

"My favorite is *Notes from Underground*, the underground man is a favorite character, the gambler is short and sweet. I love *Brothers Karamazov*. His life story is incredibly fascinating," Lily said rapidly.

Stevie looked around the glamorous, old-world space more and noticed the agent-looking dude who commandeered the booths talking loudly to himself. She could only assume he was wearing AirPods or some other Bluetooth-type device. Typically she would've turned her attention back toward Lily but eavesdropping on this shallow guy's one-sided conversation was amusing as hell:

"So, I passed out."

Pause.

"No, don't you pretend like Shitcago is NYC and there are Chinese places open at 1 in the morning. ChiCafe doesn't seem like a real name for an all night al dente al Chinese place."

Pause.

"Chinese food here is greasy and in China, it's not. Still yums?"

Pause.

"I make great Crab Rangoon. From scratch. My brother throws a pretty good Frymas party after Thanksgiving. Everyone wears pajamas and fries things. Last Frymas, my Crab Rangoon was on point!"

Even longer pause.

"Nah, I'm dumb like that. I can eat a little but a lot kills me. My body is really just an instrument to carry my head from place to place."

What in the fuck was he talking about and who was he saying it to?

"What's going on in my head isn't impressing my body much."

Pause for one hot minute.

"Which of my ridiculous comments are you questioning?"

Stevie finally looked away from the guy. If he was an agent, he was the weirdest agent she'd ever seen. And what the fuck was "Frymas" all about? She decided to write it down on her notes app for her to reflect on at a different time. When she turned to grab her phone she noticed that Lily was still talking to her. Slumped almost at a 50-degree angle and played with the olive in her drink...

"Yeah, at the beginning of the year, my friends did this shamanism healing ritual. We went to a karate dojo, near People's Park, brought sleeping bags and pillows... dressed in pajamas and depended on underwear, while holding lined popcorn buckets we'd be puking in."

She slightly trailed off and on, "And then this

one guy Bigsby aka Jack Fadell laid out a thought-provoking narration and introduction to the shaman, Nina. We had to prepare for the ceremony by fasting and refraining from alcohol and spicy foods. Sexual abstinence was demanded. There they had, they had, music. Music, dancing, and M. Night Shamanistic prayers."

Stevie downed her second martini and listened to this endless entertainment. It's like she didn't even have to be there. Lily didn't need to know her. Webster didn't need to know her. Agent-dude didn't need to know her. The three of them didn't need to know each other. It was just a kind of third place that they all happened to be at.

"So we blasted off harder than Jim Morrison or Jimi Hendrix...we broke on through. OH! And dance parties. And finger painting," Lily whimsically drew circles and stars on the bar with her ring finger with a splash of vodka she probably spilled while rambling off to nobody.

Her voice was slowly coming to a lull, "It was just pure. Purely, pure. Just real, honest to god, psychoanalysis from totally unqualified sources. It's mostly about making the most blatantly obvious observation regarding the most universally shared life experience, and emphatically hitting each word with the most profound tone and an unquestionably authentic inflection. It's like the voice of Matthew McConaughey."

"That actually does sound pure," Stevie nodded while the words, *alright, alright, alright*, began to float around in her head.

A darker ambiance began to slowly take over the lounge, making it look like it was built in the '30s. It didn't feel sinister, but things amongst the pieces of furniture included ivory and silver inlays, there was a trickling sense of dread. Perhaps the lights were dimmed more or the overall detached vibe that the bartender was giving off was beginning to spread.

Webster didn't exactly look happy with his job. He hung on the other far end of the bar, cleaning an empty whiskey glass even though there were only 3 people ordering drinks and none of them were drinking anything brown. Stevie learned that looking busy was actually a trick of the trade when the bartender had nothing else to do. Made people feel more comfortable to see them doing something rather than just hanging back. She learned that from the many times she had to pick her mother up from bars after one too many drinks. Her mom would drunkenly tell her about the "famous" people she met and then how friendly the staff was or how shitty they were. Stevie vividly remembered an incident when her mom lost it at a bartender who wasn't following the trick of the trade. Stevie was 16 and had driven all the way to the valley to find her mom in a lounge similar to this one, singing You're So Vain by Carly Simon. The bartender was wearing a white t-shirt and black vest, reading *Big Sur* by Jack Kerouac. Once he spotted Stevie, he put his book down and pointed to her mom. She led her mother away from the microphone but drunken paranoia took over before they left.

Her mother had lunged toward the bartender and screamed, “Stop fucking looking at me! I knew you were a cop, yeah!?” Stevie pulled her back and led her mom out.

“He’s killing me, smalls. He’s killing me. Never trust a guy in a white t-shirt, reading Jack Kerouac. He wasn’t even making drinks. Just watched me all night,” her mom slurred.

Luckily, the agent-looking dude’s loud voice snapped Stevie back to the present. He was almost shouting into his phone now and no longer looked relaxed in his red cushioned booth.

“That seems unfair...the counters should be lower for you and your people. I never wished I was taller than I am until I started holding toddlers and their little feet were at a quite uncomfortable crotch level. I never wished I was taller than I am until I started holding toddlers and their little feet were at a quite uncomfortable crotch level. Those are not toddlers! Those are teenagers. From my experience, they don’t like being picked up. I’m not feeling alright today...”

He slowly drifted into silence, likely listening to whatever the person on the other side was saying.

He sighed, “I’m not feeling that great. I’m not catching on fire today. Love has started to fade. I’m not going to smile today. I’m not gonna laugh. You’re out living it up today.

I’ve got dues to pay.”

Stevie couldn’t decide whether he came up with that on the spot or he was reciting words from a poem or something. Either way, the man looked sapped of all energy. He had sweat through his form-fitting suit and was drinking what looked like a martini.

As a musician, she was in shock over the fact that he was speaking so quickly without losing his breath. He was frantic, "What are you waiting for in this room of yours upstairs with your one-uppers? Suicide is a bad life choice. "Choose Designer lingerie, in the vain hope of kicking some life back into a dead relationship. Choose handbags, choose high-heeled shoes, cashmere, and silk, to make yourself feel what passes for happiness. Choose an iPhone made in China by a woman who jumped out of a window and stick it in the pocket of your jacket fresh from a South-Asian firetrap. Choose Facebook, Twitter, Snapchat, Instagram and a thousand other ways to spew your bile across people you've never met. Choose updating your profile, tell the world what you had for breakfast and hope that someone, somewhere cares. Choose looking up old flames, desperate to believe that you don't look as bad as they do. Choose live blogging, from your first wank till your last breath; human interaction reduced to nothing more than data. Choose ten things you never knew about celebrities who've had surgery. Choose screaming about abortion, choose rape jokes, slut-shaming, revenge porn, and an endless tide of depressing misogyny. Choose 9/11 never happened, and if it did, it was the Jews. Choose a zero-hour contract and a two-hour journey to work, and choose the same for your kids, only worse, and maybe tell yourself that it's better that they never happened. And then sit back and smother the pain with an unknown dose of an unknown drug made in somebody's fucking kitchen. Choose an unfulfilled promise and wish you'd done it all differently. Choose never to learn from your own mistakes. Choose watching history repeat itself. Choose a life. Choose a job. Choose a career. Choose a family. Choose a fucking big television. Choose washing machines, cars, compact disc players, and electrical tin openers... Choose DIY and wonder who the fuck you are on a Sunday morning. Choose sitting on that couch watching mind-numbing, spirit-crushing game shows, stocking junk food into your mouth. Choose to rot away at the end of it all, pishing your last in a miserable home, nothing more than an embarrassment to the selfish, fucked up brats you spawned to replace yourself, choose your future. Choose life... But why would I want to do a thing like that?"

That definitely sounded a lot like a monologue from a movie she had watched when she was younger. She'd typically shirk it off if it didn't suddenly occur to her that this kind of hotel was exactly the kind of place where people went to commit suicide or take drugs or maybe even murder people. With that thought in her mind, she couldn't understand why the sweaty alpha wannabe was just sitting there. Did he have someone he loved sitting upstairs doing drugs? Were they going to kill themselves? Why would he be down there, talking on the phone to someone upstairs?

All of those seemed like fair questions until she remembered that her therapist told her once to go to a separate location if you're in the middle of a fight with her partner. Stevie and Alfie were having a lot of fights before they broke up. She wanted to keep the relationship from dying and begged the therapist for any advice and that's what she was given. She was to tell Alfie that whenever they were about to have a fight that they should stop and go into separate locations for a previously agreed-upon amount of time. After that time passed, they were supposed to come back to each other and hopefully discuss their problem calmly. The time and separation were supposed to allow the person to come down from their anger and begin to think of the problem rationally. After Stevie got this advice she immediately told Alfie. Alfie half-agreed but never followed through. They went on fighting like they always had and eventually broke up over the tiniest of transgressions.

Perhaps that was what was happening with the agent guy and whoever he was speaking to. Maybe it was his wife or girlfriend upstairs in a room they got for the night and they began to fight over something she'd never know. Maybe one of them got the same advice and calmly departed to mull over their problem. He went down to the "Cecil Lounge" and she stayed upstairs in a room that likely matched the rest of the hotel's aesthetic. Stevie imagined a disheveled blonde woman on a hotel bed with a canopy and dark linens. The walls would be dark and all the furniture would likely be just as distressed as her. Stevie imagined the woman drinking cheap champagne rolled in from room service, hiding out from the world in a small space with heavy curtains covering the windows.

Just waiting for her partner to come back.

Stevie could tell that the agent-looking dude wasn't initially talking to her when she entered the lounge. He looked almost aloof, all spread out in a booth, likely talking to a friend from Chicago it seemed. If he and his partner had been following that sage relationship advice that Stevie was once told, they clearly broke protocol by talking on the phone. Perhaps the woman called him because he was gone for too long. Or he called her because he was still pissed and wanted to start the fight up again.

Stevie had no way of knowing. Between the two calls, she had been half-listening to Lily talk about shamans and finding enlightenment through drugs. When she wasn't listening to that she was observing the space, the sad look on Webster's face, and imagining what kind of person built this hotel.

But now all attention was on this private call that definitely had something to do with suicide. He mentioned something about a bathroom. The woman might be mixing pills and champagne with a razor blade in a clawfoot bathtub next to an outdated sink or toilet.

It was definitely the kind of thing she could write a fucked up song about, she thought as agent guy sprang up and ran to the manually operated elevator with no "elevator man" to carry him to his desired floor. He tried closing the metal grill door and operating the contraption himself but was left befuddled, so he pivoted to the stairs instead.

At that moment, Stevie was handed her fourth

martini by Lily who had apparently been explaining Sartre to her that whole time, "*Nausea* is really interesting, Sartre takes you into a mind that is slowly losing touch with reality. Strangely it's absolute freedom that causes this individual to break away from the world. Sartre famously stated that 'freedom is the ultimate condemnation' or 'we are condemned to be free'."

Stevie was struck by how on-point that talk was. Of course, she knew Sartre and had read *Nausea* before. The message she got from it was how hollow and trite life could be. She immediately told Lily about her observations and the assumption that there might be a woman upstairs killing herself as they spoke.

"Fuck, what a world it has become," Lily said while still casually drinking.

"It's a sad world," Stevie said while looking at her weirdly. "Should we be doing something? Like getting help or whatever?"

Lily looked like she didn't even hear her while gesturing to Webster to pour her another drink.

"I wonder what would make a person take that action. Maybe it's just that feeling of discomfort in doing it at their own home?" Lily mused while Webster poured her drink out of the tumbler that he shook with no effort at all.

Stevie couldn't believe it. The only thing that Lily was curious about was why a person would kill themselves in a hotel. Not the actual action of them potentially killing themself.

Lily took another sip while pushing Stevie's glass

in front of her, "You said he looked like an agent? I bet she was an actress. You think?"

Stevie just blankly answered, "Maybe."

"Then maybe it's just some natural evolution in Hollywood where self-preservation should be sacrificed in order to achieve true, everlasting fame. These people wanna become pop culture icons but don't actually want to do the level of hard work and dedication it takes to get there. Instead, they just give up their life in the pursuit of becoming the next Marilyn Monroe or something. If you think about it, it's not exactly an original idea. The only flaw is that they need to be somewhat famous first."

Stevie just sat there and drank silently. This clearly wasn't the first time Lily has seen something like this happen at the hotel. She wasn't ignoring it or trying to make herself numb to the idea of it. She just looked purely indifferent.

"You're kinda famous, right?" Lily looked at her.

Fuck, she had been chilling that whole time thinking she was drinking away her own tormented thoughts in total anonymity.

"I don't know about famous. But I am a musician," Stevie said, accepting the situation that was happening upstairs. Whatever they were. She felt calm about the fact that she didn't see any paramedics rushing up there and became indifferent about it like Lily. It wasn't her business.

"I always wonder about you musicians and dating. It's gotta be an endless supply," Lily looked at her laughing.

It was a weird pivot but Stevie was willing to move on to a less morbid subject.

"How so?" she downed her martini and slammed it down in a way that showed she was wanting another.

"You could probably just stay home, and text a guy over any hour of the day, it probably turns into some strange dopamine, chasing the dragon scenario," Lily took the drink that Stevie was given.

It was nice really to see a complete stranger cutting her off.

"You probably don't need to go out to places like here like the rest of us normies. You can hang with friends and just wait for someone to fall into your lap," Lily took a sip out of the drink that was originally meant for Stevie.

Maybe Lily wasn't cutting her off out of concern but out of intrigue about Stevie's life and knew if she got too drunk the conversation wouldn't go anywhere.

"Interesting," Stevie said, having no idea where Lily was going with this. The only thing she could assume was that Lily was trying to find someone to hook up with but was failing.

"Like I'm sure you people like you use it like heroin," Lily laughed.

"I'm intrigued by this hypothesis," Stevie only thought about Alfie. She'd never actually used her fame or music to help her date. She just wanted someone who felt like home.

"It's probably amazing," Lily went on. " It's a strange fascination for me. Like heroin. But it's probably hell trying to find a shrink if it gets out of line.

'Doc, I'm going through some groupie withdrawals.' It's probably a common paradigm in your line of work though. Right?"

Stevie ordered another drink, "I wouldn't know. I guess I'm what some people might call a 'serial monogamist.' Always in a long-term relationship with someone I truly connect with or depressed when I don't have that someone."

She lost count of how much she drank but had become fascinated by the idea that someone as risque as Lily would be having issues finding someone.

Inside you time moves

Stevie slowly opened her eyes, wincing at the pounding in her head. She groaned and reached for her phone, hoping to check the time. As she did, she noticed a barrage of missed messages and calls from her friends and family. She rubbed her eyes and looked around the room. It was a typical hotel room, with a queen-sized bed, a dresser, a TV, and a small table with two chairs. The curtains were drawn, casting a faint red glow throughout the room. It all felt so surreal.

Stevie got up from the bed and stumbled towards the bathroom. She looked in the mirror and was shocked by her appearance. Her eyes were bloodshot and her hair was a mess. Stevie splashed some water on her face and tried to collect her thoughts.

She went back into the room and sat on the bed, confused. Stevie tried to piece together what had happened the night before. She vaguely remembered drinking at the bar with the lounge pianist, a woman named Lily, but everything else was a blur.

As Stevie sat up, she noticed that she was in a hotel room that she didn't recognize. It was dark, with heavy curtains blocking out the light. She quickly checked her pockets for her wallet and ID, relieved to find that they were still there.

Stevie's phone buzzed again, and she groaned as she saw that it was the drummer in her band, Dustin Evy, calling her. She answered, her voice hoarse.

"Stevie, where the hell are you? We've been trying to reach you all night!"

"I...I don't know," Stevie stammered. "I woke up in a hotel room, and I have no idea how I got here.

I mean, I know how I got to the hotel. I just don't remember getting a room."

There was a long pause on the other end of the line before Dustin spoke again.

"Stevie, are you okay? Do you need us to come get you?"

Stevie shook her head, even though he couldn't see her. She knew that "us" meant the rest of her band. They clearly had waited long enough for Stevie to make a decision about whether she wanted to tour if they'd been trying to call all night. She couldn't remember if she told them if she was going to have an answer for them by the end of the week or whether she just told herself that.

"No, I think I'm okay. I just need to figure out what happened."

As she hung up the phone, Stevie noticed a note on the nightstand next to her. It read: "Welcome to the Hotel Xavier. Please enjoy your stay."

Stevie's heart sank as she realized she couldn't remember anything from the night before other than talking about things like "La petite mort," her mother's condo, and something about a garbage disposal.

She also remembered Webster telling her that he 'appreciated her discerning lack of enthusiasm' after she and Lily heard that no suicide had happened that night.

Her relief was short-lived though once it occurred to her that if her band was trying to call her, maybe her other friends were too. When you're drunk, it becomes almost irresistible not to give your phone a quick check: a friend in another country may have just had a baby, or someone you vaguely know might have a new opinion on a change in direction in the nation's foreign policy.

Stevie then began to worry about Twitter. It promised access to people who are so much less tricky than those in close physical proximity. Humans you have known for years get judged against angels we have yet to spend a real-life minute with on there. It could be addicting. Even if you aren't famous. At her most vulnerable moments, Twitter and social media like that, promise us that they will be able to locate your tribe amongst the vast expanse of digital waves.

So Stevie hurriedly checked her phone again and saw that she had drunk-texted a bunch of people, including her ex-boyfriend and her boss. No Twitter thankfully. But she did cringe at the messages she had sent. Especially the ones to her ex-boyfriend, Alfie...

Are we ever going to hang out? Or are we just gonna be strangers now?

We don't have to be strangers. I'm free tomorrow. What did you wanna do? Or did you mean hang out as in something in the future?

Cool. Let's see a movie.

Ok??? What movie?

idk. I'll check Secret Movie Clu later to see what they've got going on.

Cool. I can pick you up when you get off work.

No. It's cool, meet you at the theater.

Alright, just meet me at the theater I guess?

Remember when we used to get sushi before movies?

We can get some if you want. Let me know whenever the movie is showing. We can grab sushi an hour or so before the shoe.

Cool

You don't need to check the site. A movie we both love is playing tonight. I just bought the tix.

I was thinking we'd pay for our own tickets because you don't want me anymore.

???

No worries. I'll buy sushi or popcorn or something...

Stevie groaned as she scrolled through the rest of her text messages from the night before. She had a few too many drinks, and now she was regretting it. She couldn't believe the weird as fuck things she had texted to people. Luckily she didn't message the band. But she did accidentally make plans for the night with Alfie. It was all so fucked but it could've been worse.

She needed to get out of the hotel and get home before she did anymore damage.

She grabbed her phone and quickly typed out a message to her friend Finn.

"Hey, Finn, can you pick me up at the Hotel Xavier? I think it's downtown. I had a little too much to drink last night and I need to get out of here before

I do anymore damage."

She hit send and waited anxiously for a response. Finn was always reliable, and she knew he would come to her rescue.

A few moments later, her phone beeped with a new message.

"Sure thing, Stevie. I'll be there in 15 minutes. Are you okay?"

Stevie breathed a sigh of relief. She knew she could count on Finn to take care of her.

She quickly replied, "Thanks, Finn. Yeah, I'm okay. Just feeling a little embarrassed about some of the things I did last night."

Finn responded with a laughing emoji. "Don't worry about it, Stevie. We've all been there. I'll be there soon."

Stevie felt a wave of gratitude wash over her. She was so lucky to have someone like Finn who didn't judge her for her mistakes. She quickly gathered the few items she had from the night before, ran back to the bathroom to clean herself up a bit more, and headed down to the lobby to wait for Finn.

When Finn arrived, he greeted her with a warm smile and a hug. "Ready to go home, Stevie?"

Stevie nodded, feeling a little sheepish. "Yeah, let's get out of here before I humiliate myself anymore."

Finn led her to his car and helped her into the passenger seat that she had grown so accustomed to being in for so many years of dashing with him. As they drove away from the Hotel Xavier, Stevie felt a sense of relief wash over her. Her hell night was over.

WE'VE SEEN HOW STRANGE
THINGS CAN GET AT NIGHT

Stevie felt drained from the long night she had. Her head was pounding and her limbs felt heavy as she tried to get comfortable in Finn's car.

She pulled down the visor to look at herself in the mirror, knowing that her hair was a mess and her makeup was smudged. There was only so much she could do in the hotel's bathroom without a hairbrush or makeup. She carried a backpack at all times but for some reason never managed to have the right items with her.

Charger: Yes.

Leaves Of Grass: Yes.

Xanax: Yes.

Eyeliner: No.

Tums: Yes.

Winter hat: For some reason, yes.

Hair product of any kind: No.

Stevie took a deep breath and tried to gather herself. Pulled the hat from her bag and put it on so she wouldn't look totally pathetic. Hopefully, if anyone saw them driving by, they'd think she was just a hipster and not some disheveled wreck of a human being. Not that someone can't be both.

Finn looked over at her as she got settled in, almost like he was looking into her eyes for permission to head out. She just nodded her head up and plugged her phone into the Aux in his car. It was actually just a USB cord that connected her phone to the car, but the phrase "Pass the Aux" never went out of style for her. Fuck, she didn't even use a USB chord in her car to play music. She just did it via Apple CarPlay. But Finn couldn't fathom not having some form of physical connection to the music that was playing in his car, so he strictly forbade it.

As they pulled away, relief washed over her and she breathed deeply. Something about the cool morning air gave her a sense of freedom and release. Finn had come to her rescue, as he always did. Now they were on their way home, driving through the winding roads of Wherever, LA.

To pass the time, Stevie jumped around a variety of Spotify playlists on her phone, but nothing really caught her attention until she heard the opening *Hollywood Nights* by Bob Seger from her "Night Drives ☾" playlist.

"Oh, I love this one!" Finn smiled and turned up the volume. It was the first thing he said after picking her up. Stevie couldn't help but imagine how much of an inconvenience this probably was. He was probably still in bed and was woken up by the buzzing of his iPhone. Plus, he got there fast which could only mean that he probably just grabbed his keys, threw on shoes, his hoodie, and rushed out the door. She timed it. According to Google Maps, it takes close to 10 minutes to drive there. He honest to fuck got there in 15 minutes. That meant cutting out eating or going to the bathroom. Just woke up and rushed out the door. If she didn't feel so guilty about the whole thing, she'd probably be impressed by how fast he was. She didn't even consider other factors like traffic or finding parking. But that must be the benefit of being a Dasher. Always knowing shortcuts and where to find a space for your car.

They listened to the Bob Seger song in silence, lost in the guitar riffs and drifty lyrics. It was one of those songs that had the power to transport you to another place and time. It made her think of LA in the Chippendale's days. She didn't know why. She could imagine it was the kind of song you'd listen to in a Pontiac Firebird after doing coke with glammed-up friends in a shady nightclub.

As the song ended, Stevie glanced over at Finn. She enjoyed the feeling of the wind blowing through the open windows. The hotel was stuffy and isolating, so this was just the change of scenery she needed in order for her to bounce back into everyday life. One where she didn't need to think about a potential suicide or have a weirdly fatalistic conversation with a lounge singer. Then again, if she goes on tour and becomes almost more famous, those kinds of situations could become routine.

But that was a thought that Stevie didn't want to have at the moment. Instead, she wanted to be in the "here and now" with Finn. He looked so relaxed, his hands on the wheel, his eyes focused on the road, and an overall calming vibe. She was grateful for his kindness. Finn was the true definition of a "ride or die" friend. Stevie couldn't even think of who else she would've called in that scenario. Typically she was the one grabbing her mother from circumstances like that. Weeks ago she could've called someone from the band. Months ago she could've called Alfie. And sometime in the future, maybe she might be able to call Claire... if she ever feels the need to humiliate herself like that again, that is.

The next song on her playlist began: *Time in a Bottle* by Jim Croce. But the volume of it was slowly getting lower. At first, Stevie thought there was something wrong with Finn's car radio but then noticed him clicking the volume button down on the steering wheel. A pretty cool feature that allowed him to not take his eyes off the road for even a second.

"So are we gonna talk about it?" Finn asked while waiting for Stevie to answer.

Stevie just sat quietly in the passenger seat, staring out the window. Both were refusing to look at each other in the politest way possible.

"There's nothing to talk about. I'm hungover. I needed a ride home," Stevie looked down, not wanting to meet his gaze. She knew that he'd be worried about her, and she didn't want to burden him with her problems. They weren't even really problems anyways.

Then out of nowhere, he scoffed, clearly frustrated with her silence and the way she was avoiding eye contact. He could see that she was slowly spinning out. She just wouldn't admit it. It would make her feel too much like her mother. The only difference was that she still had a hopeful life ahead of her with people who actually cared about her and she cared about even more. She hadn't burned her whole world down *yet*.

The silence in the car was becoming heavy, and the only sound was the hum of the engine and the soft "Dad Rock" coming from Stevie's iPhone. Finn kept glancing over at her, worried about what was actually going on in her mind at the moment.

After a few minutes, Finn spoke up again. "Stevie, if something's bothering you, you know you can talk to me about it, right?"

Stevie sighed and turned to face him. "I know, Finn. It's just...I don't know."

Finn nodded briefly and then suddenly shook it off like her words caused a shiver down his spine. Instead of letting it go like Stevie thought he was going to do, he pulled over to the side of the road.

"Look, this car isn't going anywhere until you decide whether you wanna finally talk about this shit. No pivoting. No bullshit. What's going on with you?"

If he was trying to come off as an assertive person who could bully someone into talking to him, he wasn't pulling it off. Instead, he looked more like a concerned brother who hit some sort of emotional wall and was begging for help. Stevie put her knees up on the dashboard and groaned.

"You're really gonna push this?"

"Yeah," he said, putting the car in park. He started to readjust his seat and prepared to wait for a while until Stevie turned back to him.

"I'll talk if we keep driving. I don't like the pressure of you just staring at me, waiting for an answer like some sort of authority figure," She almost laughed saying this since there was no way in hell Finn could ever be such a person. This pressure move that Finn had just attempted actually cheered her up a bit. She needed a break from taking life too seriously.

"How about we just drive around aimlessly and we'll talk. You don't need to start heading for my apartment until we feel some form of closure about all of this," She told him. She picked her words carefully since Stevie didn't want anyone to think she was in need of any emotional rescuing on her end and she wanted to maintain some form of control over the situation as well.

"Deal," he smiled at her.

Stevie sighed and chilled back in her seat. In another life, Finn would probably make a good therapist. Not a stuffy one. He'd be more open and more amusing like Robin Williams in *Good Will Hunting*. A therapist who genuinely wants to help you but is willing to be whatever you need them to be until you feel ready to open up.

Finn slowly made his way out of the downtown bustle of LA where they had stayed parked for what seemed like an eternity. They bypassed the skyscrapers and busy streets. The more they drove the more sprawling the city outside became. It wasn't until they began to go west on the Santa Monica freeway that she realized that Finn was probably heading for the Pacific Coast Highway, also known as Highway 1. They'd be far from the grungy urban center that he picked her up from and on the coast instead, hugging the ocean and beach towns.

It was rather genius actually, since Finn knew that the only thing that allowed Stevie to sleep was her Alexa playing ocean sounds. Something about the ebbs and flows of the water soothed her. Even her therapist picked up on this and they worked on visualization exercises using that thought to help her through anxiety episodes or traumatic memories. They'd tried almost everything else in therapy before trying something as basic as a grounding exercise. EMDR, IPT, DBT, and even microdosing on LSD. But it was the sound of water that helped pull her through the best. The IPT and DBT seemed to have no effect on her. The LSD only made her more anxious. And EMDR made her despise the color purple and the sound of beeps. Finn was her closest friend aside from Dustin, so he knew all of this. Yes, she considered Dustin and the rest of the band as part of her tribe but she wasn't ready for them to know her that intimately. Even though she got shaky before each show and her songs were wracked with torment, she was desperate for at least a few people she interacted with constantly to not see her as a basket case.

One could describe the band dynamic as one similar to an overwhelmingly big family. A somewhat normal one that didn't consist of siblings hating each other or toxic parents. They supported each other like they were one unit and were open about their feelings, but they never got too deep into them. They needed to maintain certain boundaries or else toxicity could slowly seep into their vibe.

All of these thoughts made Stevie feel like she could slowly speak about the tour with a person who had no stake in it whatsoever. Someone who would support any decision she made and rooted more for her mental health than fame.

Stevie looked up at Finn for a hot minute and then poured out everything that she'd been keeping to herself, "My anxiety reached a peak last week.. It's like everything, all these expectations, just came crashing down on me. And that second album, the one that used to excite me? That idea is now suddenly a commitment and you know how I am with commitments. I used to have visions about filling it with songs, continuing the stories from 'Whispers In the Wind.' But now? I can't find those songs; it's like they're hiding in some other dimension that my brain no longer has access to. And whenever I get close, I abandon it. Everything is just slipping by. I've been trying so, so hard to write, you know? To let the music flow like it used to. But instead, it's become this constant battle, a fight against endless distractions that just leave my thoughts all scattered and incomplete. Time itself feels so weird like it's twisted and distorted, and every minute drags on forever. The agony of waiting, it's everywhere – whether I'm at the record store, waiting for time to pass, or waiting for messages from the band. It's a constant reminder of this creative standstill I'm stuck in. And, I can't help but wonder if it's all connected. My struggles, this... this fucked up-ness, is it linked to whatever is wrong with my mom and her mental health issues? Is this some kind of legacy I never wanted but somehow got stuck with? I mean, I am fucked, okay? But I don't think I'm crazy. When I'm with you, with the people who get it, it's like a tiny break from all the chaos that I've been keeping to myself. But when you aren't there I just sit in bed feeling apprehensive about everything. I guess one of the main things I've been thinking about lately is that I don't feel like I'm strong enough emotionally to motivate *slash* propel myself through this life even though I love it and I am faltering in my ability to justify why I'm even doing it. Sleep should be an escape, right? A sanctuary from the madness. But even in my dreams, anxiety just sneaks in, turning my sleep into a living nightmare. There's no escaping it; it's like a shadow that won't let go. It's like I'm just sinking. Sinking into bed, drowning in this overwhelming fear and doubt that just keeps crashing over me. There's no reprieve. You have no idea what it feels like to have found your people and to be constantly at the fringe of losing them. So I shut you all out for a night. Tried to go to a place where no one knew me. It eventually led me to the hotel and I guess that's everything. You're what's keeping me from completely falling apart."

Stevie was almost at the point of tears but also felt a huge weight thrown off of her shoulders. She let it all out. Stevie had been drowning and finally came up for air. As she leaned out the window, taking in the fresh ocean air, Finn sat in silence. It was like he was in a fugue state. She took all of her mental health issues and dumped them on him. It was a complete onslaught of problems that he wasn't prepared to hear at all. No primer. No "Finn, let's talk," and no "Okay, here's the problem." Just a deluge of almost indecipherable emotion instead. He was struggling to look at the road and figure out which problem of hers to tackle first. Finn knew she was struggling but processing every single thing she just said seemed impossible. With every second he didn't speak, Stevie's heart pounded. It felt like Dustin and his drum kit was beneath her chest, playing harder and harder. Stevie pulled herself back up and just looked out at a vast, empty horizon. She visualized herself drowning again. It felt preferable. Like coming up for air wasn't worth it. It didn't save her. It was a microsecond of relief and soon she'd be pulled back under. Stevie desperately wanted to take back every word she let spill out of her mouth.

Finn fumbled with his words, "You aren't on the fringe of losing anybody. We all support you. Why do you think Claire came over the other day? People care about you. What is it you say, you were looking for your tribe? Well, we're right here. I'm in the corner of the venue cheering you on with every new song you write and I'm hanging in the hills with you almost every time you feel stir-crazy and don't wanna sleep. I know everything is coming at you fast. Everyone handles it differently. You don't see fame. You see pressure. I can't even tell if the pressure you're feeling is because you're afraid that you won't live up to some image or whether it's disappointing us. But I can promise you, the second thing would never happen."

Stevie nodded with acceptance, watching the morning sun cast a warm glow over the coast as they drove by.

Even though the music was turned down, they filled the car creating a tranquil atmosphere. The coastal breeze gently swept through the open windows, carrying with it the scent of the nearby ocean.

The Pacific Coast Highway stretched out before them and Stevie began to think of it as a metaphor for her life, hugging rugged cliffs but offering the view of something sparkling below. It looked majestic.

Finn kept his eyes on the road, occasionally stealing glances at Stevie, who seemed lost in her thoughts. They were vast and powerful, but also calm and serene. It seemed that she'd always be dueling between these two frames of mind.

Stevie had listened attentively, finding solace in his words before but the tension in her shoulders only ease, and her breathing became steadier after almost an hour of driving and watching the rhythmic crashing of the waves. It had provided a gentle and comforting soundtrack that made her think of meditation apps. She began to think more about the album that she had been working on. How much it lacked the natural flow of the ocean below. It was forced and full of ideas that she thought people would like to hear. Instead, she wanted her lyrics to sound like those crashing waves. Strong and broken at the same time.

The salty air wrapped around them, carrying each thought she had with a gentle breeze. With her eyes fixed on the horizon, she finally decided to tell Finn more about the abysmal music she had been working on. It was no longer poetic or pure. Every word and idea was coming from a place of anxiety. Like a school project that one procrastinates on until the last minute and then speeds through at least having something to turn in. All she had wanted to do was to hand something into the band for them to offer to their growing audience and to make her mom just shut up, even if it were for just a little bit.

"I did write something," Stevie admitted to Finn, wincing.

He slowly pulled over and asked her to tell him more.

She stepped out of the car and sat on the rail next to the road, "It's really cringe. The album doesn't even have a title yet but the songs do and the names alone are enough to make someone want to burn it."

"They can't be that bad," Finn laughed, walking toward her to sit on the rail as well. "But if you hate them and they even make you cringe, don't do it. Be you. Write what you know and people will either love it or hate it. Just remember, they're only a fan of Electric Dust because of the words you wrote. And the fact that Dustin is the perfect specimen and drums shirtless. It helps. But in the end, it's your words. The one you wrote when you weren't trying to impress anyone. So write something like that."

"The band wants an answer about the tour. We have to release a new album and promote it before we leave. I texted Dustin telling him that the whole band should meet for coffee tomorrow, right before you picked me up at the hotel. You legit expect me to start over and write something entirely new?" She looked at him like he was crazy.

"I don't know. Maybe not something new. I loved that song you sang the other day to Claire and me. Maybe do something like that? Write about this last week. It seems like you've really been going through it. People might relate. But I don't know music. Only you know what's worth writing about. It's a shame that you didn't go through some intense adventure or a tragedy didn't happen," he laughed again but in a loveable way. Ride or Die friend for the win again.

That entire week was a tragic adventure in her mind. She was really going through it. Just because she wasn't going anywhere or doing anything extreme didn't mean people would be bored. Fuck, wandering the city alone could provide enough content for an entire career. She looked down at her notes app on her iPhone and nodded.

"Alright, I'll see if I can do it. I can't write an entire album before tomorrow though. I'm meeting Alfie later tonight for sushi and a movie," she said looking away.

"Alfie?!" Finn laughed even more. "How the fuck did that even happen?"

Stevie jokingly shoved him off the rail.

"I told you..." She dragged it out and groaned. "I got really drunk last night and did some texting. Some of it people ignored. One of them wasn't. I legit somehow managed to make feasible plans."

"So are you two...?" he looked at her.

"No. No... I don't think so. You think?" Stevie looked over at him as they headed back over to the car.

"I have thoughts," Finn giggled as he got back into the car.

"What?" Stevie quickly joined him so they could get out of there. Maybe getting out of there could get her out of that conversation.

"I think there's still love there," Finn started the car and pulled away. "I don't know. Don't write it off but also be prepared for it to be a strictly friends thing. I don't know. Did he sound excited?"

"It was via text douchebag! How the hell should I know? He could've just been up late last night and agreed to it because he felt sorry for me or something."

"That is a possibility as well," Finn stared at the road while turning Stevie's playlist back up.

Fast Car by Tracy Chapman came on.

"Well that's a mood," he said looking over at her.

"What am I supposed to do?" Stevie asked while searching the playlist for something else to play. How was it possible that so many songs she added to a "night drive" playlist had to do with love? She settled on *Hotel California* and then continued to look at Finn hoping he'd have the proper answer.

"Did he buy the tickets?" Finn asked.

"Yeah."

"Then there you go," Finn smiled.

"But I'm buying the sushi," she added.

"Well fuck, I don't know. Just put on clean clothes and act like you do with me. No mixed signals. Just two people hanging out. If he puts himself out there then you have your answer. But wait for him to say something. If he doesn't, then just try to enjoy the sushi and movie."

Stevie shrugged, accepting that she got her into this weird circumstance and it was all out of her control now. She picked up her phone to check the time and realized that they needed to head back to her place immediately if she was gonna be able to head out to meet Alfie in time though.

They were in traffic for almost another hour headed back but as they approached their exit, Finn turned down the "late night drive" music and glanced over at Stevie.

"Are you feeling better now?" he asked with a mixture of relief and still slight concern etched on his face.

Stevie nodded and smiled. "Yeah, thanks. The drive and the music and ocean and talking helped."

Finn grinned. "Wait, before you leave you've gotta tell me."

Stevie looked back at him confused.

"What were the names of the songs you wrote?" he laughed.

Stevie couldn't believe after all that talking and driving that he remembered that.

"Please..." Finn tried to do puppy eyes.

"Fuck, if I tell you, I don't wanna hear any shit about it. K?"

"Scout's honor!" he saluted.

"You don't believe in the scouts."

"Nope. They're a weird "America Fuck Yeah"

association that is breeding little dorks to be obedient to the American Capitalist Machine. But you know what I meant," Finn smiled smugly.

"Fuck....okay," Stevie pulled her phone back out and read them out loud:

-Mumbling nonsense to myself on the Megabus
-Cops killed Jesus
-Unemployed
-Worried about my mom and shit
-Gay sex kills cops
-Boys with Feelings
-Please clap
-Solidarity with prison riots
-only sadness
-less gender more peace
-shut your hipster ass up
-kill nazis on site

Finn stared straight ahead containing all laughter and looked over her shoulder at the phone. He pointed to one title, *Boys With Feelings*.

"Very lit. I love it."

He sucked at faking approval. Sticking to the truth is what he was best at. She knew he wouldn't mock her though after her mini-breakdown in the car. Stevie was actually impressed by his ability to hold in his laughter though. They sounded worse reading them out loud than they did reading them.

Finn smiled at her and went in for a hug, "Well, I'm excited to see what other songs you come up with.

The legit ones for the album that you're going to start over with."

Stevie nodded. "I can guarantee the titles will at least be better."

She hugged him back and thanked Finn for the ride and everything.

He smiled. "Anytime, Tiny Human. That's what I'm here for I think. Unless you get back to Alfie that is. Would be nice to have another guy help carry the load..."

He laughed loudly while heading back into his car, "I mean for a little person, you've got some pretty heavy baggage. I changed my mind, wear something nice tonight. Bring homeboy back again."

As Finn started to pull away from Stevie's apartment she shouted out, "Alright, alright alright. Get home, safe big guy."

He slowly took his foot off the gas, "Actually not going home. I'll be out. Not dashing. Just out. Text if you need me but try not to. You've got this."

"Gochu. Thanks for the long drive home," she said, her voice filled with gratitude and surprise that Finn actually had plans for the evening.

Finn yelled out from his car window, "Anytime, Tiny Human. You know I've got your back. Now get your little ass inside! You've got things to do. Tick tock!"

She looked at her phone again and saw the time. Stevie rushed up the shitty stairs to her shitty apartment to get ready. Her mind was torn between a hoodie or a cardigan. Either one was going to go over the *Scream* t-shirt that Alfie bought her two years ago when they decided to do a "Scream-a thon" at his place with their pillow forts and old-school popcorn they found at Target. The kind that Drew Barrymore made in the beginning of the first movie. Where each pop heightened the intensity of the scene which Stevie considered the best horror intro ever. She even tried once to make the very same popcorn at the same time as Cacey Becker (Drew Barrymore) did in the movie to see if Wes Craven got the pops right. Stevie learned that the smoke alarm would've gone off way faster in the film and she also learned that she was too short to turn her fire alarm off on her own.

As Stevie examined herself in the mirror she decided to wear her cult-leader-style glasses and cardigan over her shirt. The hoodie would look too sloppy. The cardigan made it look like she cared about her appearance but wasn't taking things too seriously. Like, she wasn't dressing how she would on a date it was a date but she was hoping he'd subtly be reminded of where she got it.

Stevie sat down and looked at her messages to see exactly what time she had to meet him. As she scrolled, her mind kept drifting to the night before. All of her muddled thoughts. Her desperate need for a drink. The weird vibe of the hotel. How she left almost just as confused as she was when she went in. Even though the vibe of the hotel was weird as fuck, it definitely had character. And its character fit her mood exactly that night.

She looked at her phone again and decided she

might have enough time to write at least one song before meeting with the band tomorrow.

LA Night

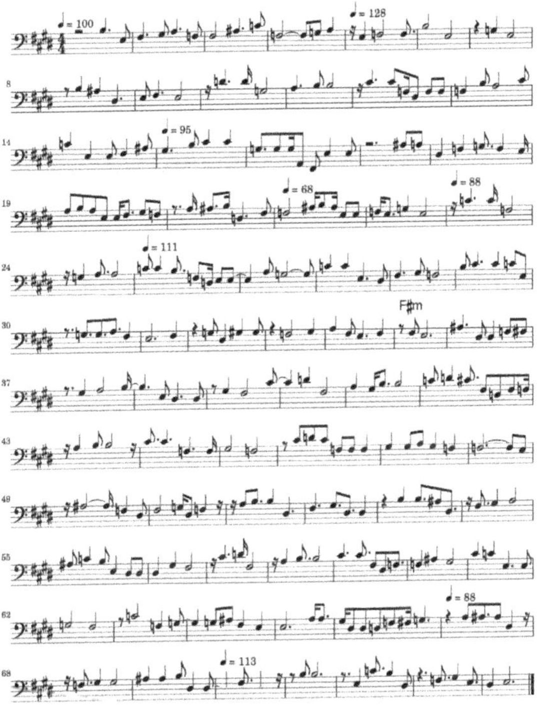

Verse 1:

She checked into the Hotel Xavier
Dead with stories, nothing could save her
The walls whispered secrets of the past
A dark history that could never last

Chorus:

Oh honey, what did you find?
In the halls, did you lose your mind?
The Elevator Man with his warning and his smoke
Did he lead you to the shadows, where the lost folks go?

Verse 2:

She took the stairs and found her room
The walls were painted in a macabre gloom
The furniture old, the curtains thick
She heard the hotel breathe and it made her sick

Chorus:

Oh honey, what did you find?
In the halls, did you lose your mind?
The Elevator Man with his warning and his smoke
Did he lead you to the shadows, where the lost folks go?

Verse 3:

Girl, she felt the weight
Of the spirits that lay in wait
She heard a knock, through her broken door
The hallway empty, but she felt a roar

Chorus:
Oh honey, what did you find?
In the halls, did you lose your mind?
The Elevator Man with his warning and his smoke
Did he lead you to the shadows, where the lost folks go?

Verse 4:
She left the hotel with a shiver
Knew she'd never be the same, not forever
The stories and the spirits stayed with her
The Hotel Xavier, where lost souls blur

Chorus:
Oh honey, what did you find?
In the halls, did you lose your mind?
The Elevator Man with his warning and his smoke
Did he lead you to the shadows, where the lost folks go?

Outro:
The hotel, a place of dark allure
She found something, something pure
A place where the dead and living meet
The hotel, where time and history repeat.

The vibe of it just felt so right. It ebbed and flowed. Was like water crashing over rocks with hints of her inner torment. And the hotel's as well. This. This would be the song she'd show the band tomorrow. She hoped they'd like it. If not, she'd probably have to show them the cringe songs she told Finn about. But Stevie felt fairly confident that this would be a decent example of what the sound of the album would be. And maybe, just maybe, she might also show them the song she wrote about Alfie depending on how she felt after their hangout. It could give the album the kind of breath that it needs.

Her phone buzzed and she saw Alfie's face show up on her screen. She was late...

I'LL JUST SIT TIGHT, IN THE SHADOWS OF THE NIGHT

Stevie gazed apprehensively at Aflie's face on her phone's screen as it continued to ring. She remembered taking the picture of him at Coachella two years back. He was sitting in the grass after he got drenched in water and beer that had rained down on him during one of the shows. Alfie was rocking a vintage Neil Young t-shirt that he bought from some artist he found on Instagram and worn-out denim shorts. It was around twilight when she snapped the picture. The mixture of the lighting fixtures on the stages and the kaleidoscope of colors captured the mood of the show. He looked so tired but euphoric beneath the delicate sky.

Her heart skipped a beat.

She knew that the second she answered it, she'd have to come up with an excuse about why she was late. She considered making up bullshit about traffic or running behind because of work that she hadn't even done that day. Stevie just knew that she couldn't admit that she got so caught up in herself and in her music, that for one hot second, she forgot about him. It was the focal point of many of their fights. But she took the leap and answered with no real plan on what to say.

What will be, will be. Or some shit like that.

She was immediately struck with the unique vocal timbre in his voice that was both raw and vulnerable, typically full of earnestness and introspection. Something about it had always given her a sense of intimacy and connection with him. Stevie often wondered if other people had that same feeling when they heard him speak. But it didn't matter. His raw and vulnerable voice sounded a tad frantic. It was like someone had knocked the wind out of him. He sounded half-distracted and half-neurotic at the same time, apologizing for being late.

"Fuck, fuck, fuckkk..." was all she could hear amidst honking and splashing in the background.

"Sorry, wasn't saying fuck to you. I wouldn't say fuck to you. I mean I would. But...you know what I mean. I just wanted to let you know that I'd be maybe 15 minutes late getting there."

She could tell he was stopped because she could actually hear him then.

Alfie breathed in and out heavily, "I'm riding my bike...YEAH SAME TO YOU ASSHOLE," she heard another splash and honk, "and of all the nights that we could've made plans, you picked one of the 37 times out of the year where it actually rains in L.A. But I'll be there. I promise I'll be there. Just please wait for me Yakuza. Aww fuck, the light just turned green, LOVE YOU."

She heard the splashing amplified again and the call was over.

His final words caught her off guard but then again so did the call. He knew she hated being called when she could've been texted instead. That was the joke on why she'd survive the movie, *Scream*. She never answers the phone. IFKYK. She had an even stronger dislike for the fact that he was calling while riding his bike in the rain. For a guy who was averse to technology, he had just been rather cavalier about using it. Stevie thought about how dangerous it was to be doing all of that at the same time. She hated that he biked around in Los Angeles at all. She always said he was the only dork in Los Angeles that rode a bike everywhere. It's a car city. But his cheerful demeanor always won out when they had talks like that. She'd argue for his safety. He'd argue for the Earth's safety. There was no debating him on that one. Alfie's last words were probably a mistake due to being rushed. Due to him always speaking to her like that in the past. Just an old habit. She wouldn't say anything about it. She would hurry up and rush now though. Since he was 15 minutes away she could make it in an Uber. Even if she showed up a bit late it worked out because he never actually asked where she was. She would just blame the rain too.

Stevie peered out of the window, watching as dark clouds rolled across the sky, obscuring the once-bright Los Angeles sunshine that she was in only a few hours earlier. Drops of rain splattered against the glass, leaving trails as they trickled down. With a sigh, Stevie picked her iPhone backup and checked the weather app. It confirmed her suspicions—a heavy rainstorm was expected to last for hours. Annoyingly the lyrics of that one Albert Hammond song came to the forefront of her mind. The only difference is it was her mom's voice singing it and not Albert's. The woman LOVED that song. Either way, Stevie shook it off and opened up her Uber app. She was going to try a new thing where she'd pretend that her mom never existed and just live in the here and now. No more crazy. Just action.

Her phone lagged but once she got on the app, Stevie quickly entered her destination as Yakuza Sushi and changed out of her cardigan, and put the hoodie on instead. Different weather, different wardrobe. He'd probably be soaked anyways from riding his bike in the rain like a moron. He'd get it. Besides, it wasn't a date.

She kept her phone unlocked and in front of her watching the little car icon move on the screen as it searched for nearby drivers. It was a Saturday night. Almost everyone in the damn city was probably ordering one. She sighed and sat for what she thought would be forever. Moments later, the app pinged, indicating that a driver had been assigned.

As Stevie hopped up and grabbed her backpack, a notification appeared on her phone.

"Your Uber is two minutes away."

Perfect timing, she thought. She headed out the door, taking a deep breath as she stepped into the fresh smell of rain.

Stevie stood under the shelter of her shitty building's entrance, eagerly scanning the street for her ride. A sleek black car pulled up, its headlights cutting through the gloomy weather. Stevie recognized the Uber by the driver's face only and waved him over.

"Hey, are you Brian?" Stevie asked the driver as she opened the back door like she always did.

"Yep! Stevie?" the driver responded in a similar manner.

"Yes," she hopped inside, carefully enough to not get her wet feet on anything other than the floor but hurriedly enough to drop her iPhone on the floor of the car. The driver, a friendly middle-aged man greeted her with a warm smile and grabbed it for her.

"Evening to you, Miss Fischer," Brian said, his voice carrying a tinge of a Southern accent. "Where can I take you today?"

She hated whenever they asked that. Like he didn't have the name of the destination right in front of him on his phone?

Stevie sighed, adjusting her seatbelt and settling into the comfortable leather seat.

"Yakuza Sushi, please. It's downtown," she answered.

Brian nodded, "Got it. Yakuza Sushi, downtown LA," he confirmed. This guy was definitely not local and definitely new to the platform.

She sighed and scrolled through Twitter on her phone.

The rain beat hard against the windows as the car smoothly merged into the traffic.

Stevie looked out, watching as Los Angelinos hurried by, seeking refuge from the sudden storm. She couldn't help but appreciate the beauty in the chaos—the way the raindrops danced against the city lights, turning the streets into a glittering reflection.

As they approached downtown LA, Brian skillfully maneuvered through the busy streets, occasionally checking his GPS for the best route. For a guy that didn't seem local, he was doing a damn fine job. Stevie could see the glowing sign for Yakuza Sushi in the distance, and the anxiety she was feeling earlier began to swell.

"Here we are," Brian announced, pulling up in front of the restaurant. Stevie thanked him in a shaky voice and gave him his rating through the Uber app, adding a somewhat decent tip. She could never tell how much was actually appropriate but she did know he was good at what he did.

As Stevie entered the restaurant, she shook off the remnants of rain from her hoodie and then looked around to see if Alfie had beaten her there or not.

As she scanned the dimly lit space for any sign of him, she was struck by how much of a warm and intimate atmosphere it was. She'd only gone there with Alfie, so it had been quite a while since she'd set foot into the place. Her heart pounded. The familiar aroma of soy sauce and freshly prepared sushi filled her senses, transporting her back to the times when she and Alfie would sit at a private table in the corner, laughing, people-watching, and probably geeking out about whatever movie they were about to see or had just seen.

As she peered over to their usual spot she saw what looked like a husband and wife. That table belonged to them now. Perhaps it only belonged to happy couples. The place was packed, but Alfie definitely wasn't there yet. As Stevie looked at the taken booths and communal tables, she wondered how long it would take for them to get a seat or whether they'd be able to get one at all if they wanted to make it to their movie on time.

This immediately reminded her that she still didn't even know what movie they were seeing or the exact time it was. Or the location for that matter. She just trusted Alfie when he said it was perfect for her.

She took a deep breath and waited. Although the walls were adorned with traditional Japanese artwork, featuring delicate brushstrokes and vibrant colors, Stevie's gaze was drawn to the sushi bar, a focal point of the restaurant. Her eyes always made their way there. It showcased a team of sushi chefs, their hands moving with precision and grace as they artfully prepared each dish. She loved watching them make sashimi to the point where she almost wanted to order it until she remembered that she was a nigiri fan all the way.

Typically she'd be looking at them doing this while sitting in her booth, covered in soft, ambient lighting with Alfie by her side. Now she was just standing there awkwardly waiting for someone to come by so she could get seats or for Alfie to suddenly show up and take charge of the situation. For a nerdy guy, he never seemed to have issues being in control of things.

And suddenly there he was. Tight blue jeans, cuffed at the bottom with a hoodie too.

She also noticed him wearing a *Jurassic Park* t-shirt as they both fumbled trying to hug each other, "Hello." She remembered buying that for him when they saw it in 35mm a long while back. They had both been so excited since neither was old enough to have seen it in theaters when it was first released. The theater showing it even ran the original movie trailers for the '90s that went along with it.

As Stevie and Alfie pulled back from their awkward hug, they both played it off as him not wanting to get her wet. Sadly, Stevie knew that this was only the first hard-to-gauge boundary that they'd be experimenting with that night. She'd never hung out with an ex before and wasn't exactly sure of the protocol, so she just followed Finn's advice earlier.

Stayed as casual as possible in what was now an impossible situation.

After their failed attempt at a hug, Alfie went up to see if there were any seats available only to be told that they'd have to wait for maybe 30-45 minutes.

Stevie could hear him mumble "fuck" under his breath.

He skirted over to her and said, "Looks like this is the place to be tonight. The wait time is about 45 minutes."

She paused before asking what they should do.

"I've been looking forward to this place all day. The smell of sushi in the air right now is killing me. The movie is in 2 hours though. We could wait, eat quickly, and hurry to the theater..." he speculated while turning everything over in his mind.

"How far away is the theater?" Stevie pressed, hoping that it would cause him to make a decision.

"Not too far. Maybe a 20-minute Uber ride away but with the rain... I don't know."

"Would we still even make the movie?" she asked.

"Not if you want to do our usual thing. Where we first scope the place out and get a beer and candy. And then finding our favorite seats in the back would be hard if we made it there right on time. If we're late we might get stuck having to sit up front and I know you hate doing that. Hurts your neck," he said tenderly looking at her.

They both looked desperate and out of options, accepting that they'd probably just have to go to the movie early and load up on candy instead until they heard a slap.

But suddenly the people ahead of them in line got into an argument, that turned into a slap, that turned into them being asked to leave. As per usual, Stevie and Alfie dug on the drama. They dug that it made their wait time shorter, even more. The decision was made. Wait at Yakuza and do their best to make the movie on time.

"I can deal with the front row if it comes down to it," Stevie assured him.

"Plus, we've seen it a million times," he added while awkwardly trying to fit his phone into his jean's front pocket.

"So what movie is it?" She did her best to do the puppy eyes to get him to tell her.

"Those don't work on me you know," he laughed and looked away. "It's a surprise. You'll like it. I promise. The minute you messaged last night, I looked at Secret Movie Club and saw that it was showing. I knew it would be perfect. That's why I rushed to buy the tickets."

Stevie wished she remembered the night before more. She also wished she knew what Secret Movie Club was. She discreetly started Googling it on her phone and felt a nudge.

"No cheating," Alfie whispered in her ear playfully. "The lady just told me that there are seats available. Are we alright with a communal experience tonight?"

He made sure to ask her with an adorable smile on his face, trying to sell her on an idea that he knew she didn't like. She hated being too close to other people on dates because it ruined the vibe.

But this wasn't a date, she reminded herself. No vibe to ruin. He clearly felt this way she thought, or else he wouldn't suggest they sit there. Whispering in her ear felt flirty though. With each second, she hated herself more and more for going to that hotel and getting white girl wasted and then sending drunk texts.

"Yeah, I'm fine with that. Let's go," she said cooly and followed Alfie to their seats. Stevie told the waitress they were ready to order before they were even fully seated. Alfie sucked at time management and she wanted to make sure that he didn't get too lost in the atmospheric sushi place and forget that they had another place to be.

"Uhhh yeah," Alfie looked up at Stevie. "You know what you want?"

"I'm good with getting our usual, you?"

"Same."

Alfie put the menu down and quickly said the order like it was a line he had to remember for a school play.

"Alright.... uhhh Gyoza, Tempura, one Rainbow Roll, One Yakuza. Did you want something to drink?" He gestured towards Stevie. She wanted sake but didn't want to have to look at the menu and decide which sake went best with their order and then try and decide if they wanted to share sake or get their own and if he didn't want any, she'd feel awkward drinking alone...

"I'm good with water."

"Same. Water."

Their menus were taken and they were given their water immediately. The two of them both looked around the restaurant sheepishly while they waited for their food. But there was only so much sleek and modern interior design to admire. Sure, they could eavesdrop on other people but the idea of it just felt rude and it wasn't like they were physically close enough to gossip to each other about it anyway.

Neither knew what to talk about nor who would break the silence. Alfie was the one who went for it.

He fiddled with his straw, "So.... I've been reading the haiku of Buson and the haiku of Basho. Been feeling 'in the mood' for a novel though. Have you been reading anything? Got any recommendations for me?" He nervously chuckled.

At that moment Stevie felt immense relief. He was more nervous than she was. Sadly, she hadn't read anything new lately though.

She felt she had to offer him something though, "I hear that new George Saunders book is supposed to be good."

"Is it a novel or short story collection?"

"You know...I don't recall. How's life been lately?" Stevie quickly pivoted.

Alfie shrugged at the change of subject and went with it.

"Life is ok. A bunch of people I know have been getting married. It's kind of making me freak out and worry about my future. Other than that I'm basically ok. How have you been?"

She wished she didn't ask that now. But she should've known he'd be weirdly honest with her. He always was, almost to an annoying degree. But Stevie appreciated that she always knew how he felt about her and where he stood on certain things.

"Me? Just work. You know. I recently hit a stubborn streak where I don't give a fuck about the future so I'm good. Just been working a lot. Trying to work on some new songs," She hated how flustered she sounded. Took a big gulp of water.

"Yeah the future seems to be becoming more tangible for me and I guess that's what's freaking me out. Are you working on a song with the band more now or writing the songs yourself still?" He took a huge gulp of water too.

"Myself," she did her best to explain the direction she was trying to go in with the new album and even showed him the new song.

"Are you experiencing immense emotional states? Sorry if that's a weird question," Alfie asked after listening to her intently and reading the lyrics while the sushi arrived.

"A bit of a strange one," Stevie was struggling to decide which roll she wanted to start on and even stopped to consider how they were sharing things now that they weren't a couple. "But yes. Very immense emotional states."

It was weird how the two of them could just talk that way, so raw and honest. She did her best to grasp her chopsticks and moved an equal amount of each dish toward Alfie. Stevie hated how dorky she looked holding her chopsticks. She was frequently letting things slip and every time she did, she peeked up to see if anyone had noticed. Alfie would just smile and show her how to hold them. She already knew how but was out of practice since, again, he was the only person she ever got sushi with.

"Good. I mean hopefully, they're not too bummer. I try to milk intense emotional states so I can work. I know you do too. I've been feeling kinda bland a lot lately. So I've been drinking box wine to compensate and hopefully feel emotional while listening to music. But so far I just feel bland," Alfie sighed. "Your music doesn't make me feel bland though. Don't think that. I've just really been going through it. This song is perfect. No one will feel bland when it's completed."

She smiled and they discussed her music and what she was doing with it, while quickly trying to finish their food to make it to the movie on time.

She decided to throw her fear of going on tour on Alfie now. Before the meal was over and before their rhythm went away.

"I'm afraid about us going on tour. I want to play music and be happy. But the idea of having to constantly be better than I was each time I accomplish something has been causing me immense anxiety. I also don't want to lose who I am to become part of some social media strategy to promote my music."

Alfie wasn't even a little phased. He drowned his last piece of sushi in soy sauce and responded, "Sometimes I wish we lived in an ice age instead. All of this needs to be performative instead of being who you are. It isn't cool. It isn't fair to make someone you're a fan of into a product so you can consume them. You aren't a product."

When he did this, the sauce splattered a tad causing the brown liquid to land on his shirt. Alfie clumsily tried to dab it off but failed, seeming flustered and embarrassed.

He asked to see the lyrics to the new song again while he dipped his napkin in water in another attempt to get the soy sauce off of his shirt, "This is who you are. These aren't faked emotions for the sake of 'listens' on Spotify. You're bearing your heart and soul here. I wouldn't get too lost in the anxiety about touring. Remember what your therapist told you?"

Before he could finish that sentence she said it with him mockingly, "It's easier to turn anxiety into excitement instead of trying to make it go away."

He smiled and they both began to clean up after themselves by stacking their dishes on top of each other to make it easier on the waitress when they left. The two always insisted that doing this was just one of the many differences between them and Baby Boomers. Baby Boomers leave a mess and expect someone to clean it for them because it's that person's job to do that. It didn't matter if the person made minimum wage and was probably left a terrible tip. Boomers tended to expect that if they spent money on something, they were able to do whatever they wanted. Stevie began to think back to the cigarette with Finn the other night and whether this was the same kind of situation but failed to come to a conclusion.

Alfie had just broken the awkwardness again by asking about her mother.

"You're nervous about losing your identity and not disappointing your mother, right?"

"Right," Stevie said, half believing that to be true.

"Because you won't fail like her."

Stevie nodded.

"And you aren't just an extension of her who should be fulfilling her dreams..."

Stevie nodded in a more aggressive way to signal that she was done with that topic.

"I know," she finally said.

"Alright. Just because you look like her and have similar talents, doesn't mean you have to be like her. Or suffer the same fate. You're thoughtful with almost all of your actions. I see that now even more. And being spontaneous and being manic are two different things."

Stevie sighed and nodded one final time, grabbing her backpack.

"Good. Sorry to be a drip. Now are you excited to see the movie?" he stood up, placing cash on the table so they wouldn't have to wait for the waitress to collect a card and return it.

Aflie grabbed Stevie's hand and his cellphone at

the same time, leading her to the exit.

"Fuck," he said while staring at his phone.

Stevie assumed that he checked Uber and saw that the wait time for a car was ridiculous and would cause them to miss the movie completely. Impolitely, she looked over her schedule to see but saw him in the app store instead, downloading both Uber and Lyft.

She'd feel bad about peering over anyone else's shoulder or looking at their phone, but with Alfie, it was just a force of habit. Plus, he never seemed to mind.

"I am sooo sorry," he turned to Stevie, flustered and waiting for at least one of the goddamn apps to load. The WiFi there sucked and his phone had no bars. "YES, they both downloaded. Uhm, is it cool if we do Lyft? Uber is more bro-y and they crossed the picket line years ago. I can't do it. Plus, Lyft has the fun mustaches."

Stevie groaned silently to herself. She had dated him for years. She should've known that he didn't have the apps on his phone and they'd he was weird enough to take a moral stance on which one to use. He was too kind. Too thoughtful. He cared about the planet. He cared about workers' rights. If they were still dating she'd probably be grumbling something to him but she forced herself to remember the circumstance as to why they were there in the first place.

She thought back to being at Hotel Xavier. How she stumbled upon it because she felt so small but too big that night. How she wanted to just be a person and not be a commodity like Alfie had just said earlier. She vaguely recalled the lounge singer and the agent and the bartender. All seeming to search for some deeper meaning. Or at least that's what she drunkenly projected onto them.

She considered how the drunk text she sent to Alfie could've gone:

Stevie: Are you sleeping?

Alfie: I was

Stevie: What's up Alfie? Do you want to watch a movie or something? Like we used to?"

Alfie: No Stevie. We are broken up.

Stevie: Does that mean we can't watch movies?

Alfie: Pretty much. Look I need sleep. Why don't you message one of your many acolytes instead...

Alfie ghosts. She never hears from him again.

But that's now how it went. Aflie was too kind. He accepted immediately and made plans that would make her happy. She couldn't be frustrated with him. She was lucky to have ever had him in the first place.

Stevie turned to him cooly, "Let's do Lyft. Uber can be kinda douchey."

He went on the app and typed in the address for The Million Dollar Theater.

She glanced at his phone again while he waited to see what cars were in the vicinity, "By the way, they don't do the mustaches anymore. Now they have a light thing on their dashboard that says 'Lyft.' It's actually pretty cool. When it lights up it matches the color that your phone gets."

"What light?" he looked at his phone which notified him that a black Honda Civic would be there in 2 minutes. As he looked at his phone he saw the color to look out for in the car. "Nevermind. Purple."

He kept his phone out as they waited at the entrance of Yakuza, not wanting to step out yet because of the rain. The doors swung open every few minutes for more and more patrons to come into the area where they were waiting, causing the two to slowly move outside. With each step, the smell of rain and soy sauce mixed and created a unique fragrance that was unfamiliar to both of them. It wasn't bad. It was actually sweet with only a tinge of sourness.

The rain poured relentlessly over the city of Los Angeles, drenching the streets and washing away the usual hustle and bustle of the city. The two of them huddled close to each other, trying to stay warm from the chill rain. The second Alfie spotted the Honda Civic, he anxiously waved it down.

It pulled up to the curb of the restaurant and the two eagerly climbed into the backseat, grateful for the warmth and the fact that they would definitely make the movie if the driver, Carlos, didn't fuck around.

"The Million Dollar Theater?" Carlos confirmed. Stevie stopped herself from groaning while putting her seatbelt on.

"Yes," Alfie responded, giving Stevie a reassuring glance. Despite the rain, he was determined to make sure Stevie didn't miss the movie he wanted to surprise her with.

Carlos nodded and merged into the slow-moving

traffic, artfully navigating the slippery streets. As they drove through the city, Alfie and Stevie found themselves again lost in search of something to talk about. Luckily, the gentle hum of the car and the rhythmic swishing of the wipers provided a soothing soundtrack to keep the car from being completely silent. Plus, Carlos didn't talk much. Stevie always appreciated this in a driver and often wished there was a feature on these apps that allowed you to request no small talk. She knew the main thing he wasn't talking though was that his passengers looked like a couple and he probably didn't want to intrude.

Alfie, again, was the first to break the silence, but instead of starting small he just went for the question that Stevie had even been asking herself since the night before.

"So why did you message me last night? It was pretty random. Don't get me wrong...I was happy," he assured her. "But what prompted you to talk to me out of nowhere?"

He was so genuinely curious. And Stevie was so genuinely unaware of what her motivations were. She just decided to be as honest as possible without sounding like she should be hospitalized for 72 hours.

"I was out last night trying to get my head together. Must've wandered the city for hours. I finally ended up at a bar downtown. Now don't judge..." She started to remember why they broke up in the first place.

But before she could finish what she was gonna say he interjected, "I'm not. I was an idiot for ever judging you for just being normal and drinking. Just because our parents couldn't handle their lives, doesn't mean we can't handle ours. Especially you. I just got so triggered that night. I could smell the alcohol on your breath and heard you up with Isaac all night. Felt like you didn't even need me anymore. I was scared and didn't want to lose control over our relationship. Like some immature teenager, I just lashed out."

Alfie's breath deflated and he leaned his head on his window, staring out at each drop that hit the glass.

He slowly looked back up and put his hand on Stevie's, "Sorry, I made that all about me. Go on."

Stevie looked at him surprised. She was the person who always had to apologize for things in their relationship. For all of his kindness, the only thing Alfie was never capable of doing was saying he was sorry. This was the closest he ever came to it. In fact, that was him saying it in the only words he knew how.

She continued being even more honest, "To be truthful, I don't remember too much about last night. I ended up at a hotel bar talking with a shockingly depressing but amusing lounge singer and watching what looked like a guy trying to desperately save what I think was a relationship. That's what it looked like at least. There might've been a suicide attempt. Not sure. The last thing I really remember is talking about Sartre with the lounge singer and then waking up in the hotel room. I sadly don't even know what caused me to text you. I don't remember doing it."

She waited for Alfie to look hurt or be upset but he just nodded reassuringly.

"Sounds like you were really going through it.

This whole time I thought the idea of being famous didn't bother you. Like it was the goal. I never realized how much the pressure of it all was weighing on you. Do you want to go on tour? Like is it what you want? Not the band..."

He was no longer curious about why she messaged but worried about her current state.

"I think so. But based on the messages I sent, it looks like I quit my job, sent an annoying message to Dustin, and then messaged you. You were the only one I wasn't shitty to from the looks of it. I guess you were on my mind because I wrote a song about you the night before," she winced, waiting for him to be weirded out. The fact that she wrote a song about him was something she didn't want him to know and there it just flew out of her mouth.

He was smiling and intrigued.

"Can I check it out?"

And at that perfect moment, the car pulled up outside The Million Dollar Theater, its historic façade bathed in a soft glow. Alfie just smiled at Stevie and thanked Carlos warmly and stepped out onto the wet pavement. As he stood under the awning of the theater, Alfie's eyes sparkled. He knew he'd probably be able to hear the song later but at that moment the movie was the only thing on his mind. Or maybe it was Stevie in general.

She couldn't tell.

"Okay, close your eyes. I don't want you to see the name of the movie we're seeing," he whispered excitedly, his words barely audible over the sound of raindrops hitting the car door that he was opening for her.

She closed them, even though she hated to do that and he grabbed her hand, leading her into the theater. As they stepped inside, they were greeted by a grand lobby that exuded an elegant opulence. The lobby featured high ceilings, chandeliers, and luxurious furnishings.

She'd been there several times before but the classic theater always made her smile. The wall was embellished with beautiful artwork and decorative moldings, and the floor was covered with rich carpets. This was definitely the kind of theater that they'd typically go to after a sushi night. They'd either see an indie film or a midnight movie on nights like that.

After Alfie fumbled through the whole ticket situation, he started to steer Stevie toward the candy.

In that instant, she remembered her favorite dorky thing she did when they did their late-night sushi/ movie dates. Going to the bathroom and taking a mirror selfie. She loved how grunge she looked in the mirror compared to how delicate the place looked.

Alfie didn't know this because of his dislike of social media, but Stevie loved it, and every single time she used the same hashtag: Just another LA night.

He was caught off guard when she said she needed to run to the bathroom real quick.

Alfie looked toward the theater somewhat anxiously but told her to go and that he'd get the popcorn and candy.

Teamwork makes the dream work.

"Wait, Raisinets and cider beer, right?" he asked Stevie nervously before letting go of her hand.

"Yep," she said quickly, pleasantly surprised that he remembered. "Don't worry about which cider beer to grab though. I'll be quick. Angry Orchard is chill if they don't have anything cool."

She started to slowly make her way to the bathroom, nodding awkwardly to the people she passed. She'd played this game before. Act like she legit has to go there but not like she's in a hurry. Bathroom etiquette was already odd enough for girls. Sneaking in for a quick mirror selfie really required her to walk in with a proper amount of confidence. Casual but not lingering. Quick but not rude.

As usual, there were already several other girls in the bathroom when she got in there. Luckily this meant that the seats in the theater probably weren't all filled. This would infinitely please Alfie.

The girls at the mirror clearly didn't know proper bathroom etiquette and were just talking like the entire space was theirs. Stevie wouldn't be able to wait them out without looking weird unless she went to a stall.

After what felt like forever, they left. Stevie had her iPhone out, ready to quickly do a quick selfie before anyone could come in. There was something private about taking selfies even though she shared them with the world a minute later. Right before she could take it, she noticed a leggy, brunette waltz in. The second she turned around Stevie could see it was Claire. She was taken aback by how steady Claire was and the fact that she was smiling. Apparently, she didn't need to be drunk to be happy.

"Whoa, what are you doing here?" Stevie asked her, both seriously curious and also wanting to act like they were legit friends now. She wasn't even sure how much Claire remembered about that one night but Stevie remembered everything. From Claire's ex to her flirtation with Finn to the weird performances they all gave in the parking lot.

"Finn and I are checking out *Almost Famous*. He said he saw you earlier. Didn't he tell you?" she responded with a mixture of joy and surprise. Not in an erratic way like she would fall off a stool if she was on one. Instead, she was trying to keep her cool in anticipation of whatever Stevie's response might be.

"Nah, I kinda hijacked most of our hangout, so he didn't tell me. Or maybe he kind of did? You two are here...together?"

Claire smiled like a teenager, "Yep. Stevie, I am so happy we went out the other night. I was starting to feel really alone here after all that drama in my life back East. Getting lit with you two made me feel like I actually belonged. I don't know, like we were squad or something. Anyhow, Finn and I got coffee the next day and I don't know...we're here now."

Stevie kinda vibed them checking each other out the other night but was kinda blown by their fast action.

Claire scanned Stevie's face and reassured her nervously, "We're taking it slow. I don't even know if we're dating or hanging or whatever this is. I know I'm happy. That's it. I'm not some impulsive person who dives head-first into things. I think I definitely gave off that vibe the other night. I was really going through it. But again, you two helped."

Maybe tribe after all...

After a short beat, Claire looked at Stevie coyly, "Are you here on your own?"

It was Stevie's turn to blow Claire's mind a tad, "Nah, I'm actually here with...Alfie? I don't know if you remember me mentioning him. He's my ex...you know the song...I don't know. I'm here with him."

Having to explain a situation that she didn't even understand, flustered Stevie to the point where her face felt red. She waited for a reaction from Claire.

Claire just looked at Stevie, "I knew there was still something there. Just because I was drunk doesn't mean I forgot our whole hangout. Except Finn did tell me I played some arcade game with him. Is that true? But yeah, your song the other night. I could totally tell. And Finn vaguely hinted at something earlier. So you two are seeing *Almost Famous* too?"

Stevie stood still for a hot second, realizing slowly that it was one of her favorite movies and Alfie knew she'd love it. It washed over her like some strange revelation. God, he knew her too well.

Stevie laughed awkwardly, "I guess so. I have to hurry though. Alfie is getting drinks and candy and then we have to hunt for a seat."

Claire looked at her phone, "Oh fuck, you're right. The movie is gonna start in like 10 minutes. I'm gonna be right out."

"Wait what?" Stevie planned to be in there for a

few minutes. She didn't plan to run into someone and get lost in conversation.

She rushed out of the bathroom and quickly looked around to see if she could spot Alfie. He didn't text her that he got seats so he likely was just waiting around for her somewhere.

Stevie finally spotted him. He was next to Finn waiting outside of the women's bathroom awkwardly. Both chilling with snacks for themselves and their plus one. Neither of them looked like they were really talking but they still acknowledged each other's presence.

Alfie stood up the minute he saw Stevie and said, "Thank god. I saw there were some seats right at the back of the theater. I was gonna actually send Finn in there to save them for all four of us but I wasn't sure if you wanted to be alone." his voice had lowered at the second part of that sentence.

He nodded his head, gesturing to come closer, and whispered, "So when did you and that mean girl chick from the store become close? And how did that happen?"

He nodded his head in Finn's direction. Her poor friend had two large popcorns, a soda, and something bulging out of his jeans pocket. It looked like Junior Mints but she couldn't be sure.

Finn noticed Stevie and stood up too while trying to not lose any of the items he was carefully balancing.

She leaned back to Alfie, "Long story. I'll tell it later. We should get to our seats. I don't care if we all sit together."

She took her beer and candy from Alfie and started toward the theater.

"Hold up!" Claire quickly walked out of the bathroom, flustered but ready for the movie.

Finn walked over to Claire, greeting her with the snacks, and then whispered to a still amused Stevie as he passed her by, "Long story. I'll tell you later."

The four stood awkwardly, sharing amused looks as they processed the evening's serendipitous turn of events.

None of them spoke. Just waited for someone to make a move. The silence was only broken by Stevie's iPhone.

The band's GroupChat...

Alfie peered over Stevie's shoulder and said in the best deep voice he could muster, "Uhm, ladies and gentlemen, good evening and welcome to the show. At this time we ask that you turn off your phones, and please note that photography and filming are not permitted. Now, sit back, relax, and enjoy..."

Stevie looked back at him, "I'm putting it on 'Do Not Disturb' right now. See?"

She flashed her phone to all four of them, "Doing it now."

Finn and Alfie both cocked their heads, "Wwwwait. Are they asking about the tour?"

"It would appear so. I'll get back to them after the movie."

Alfie leaned over to her again, "At least acknowledge them and let them know you're alive."

Stevie sighed and thought for a bit, "Okay."

She typed quickly on the chat while looking at the theater doors hoping to make it in there on time: Tour talk. Tomorrow. Hotel Xavier. Cecil Room. 3 pm.

"Alright, everything should be good now. I'll see what they say after the movie."

A few people scampered into the theater prompting the four of them to perk up.

Alfie broke the silence, "Alright! Who's ready to go on tour with Stillwater?!" in an attempt to snap them out of it and hype them up at the same time.

Claire, who was in the dark about everything that whole time decided to go with it and immediately high-fived the dorky guy she just met, "Let's do it!"

She then lowered her voice while gesturing for them to follow her into the theater, "I mean seriously, what the fuck else is there to do on a rainy night in LA?"

iykyk

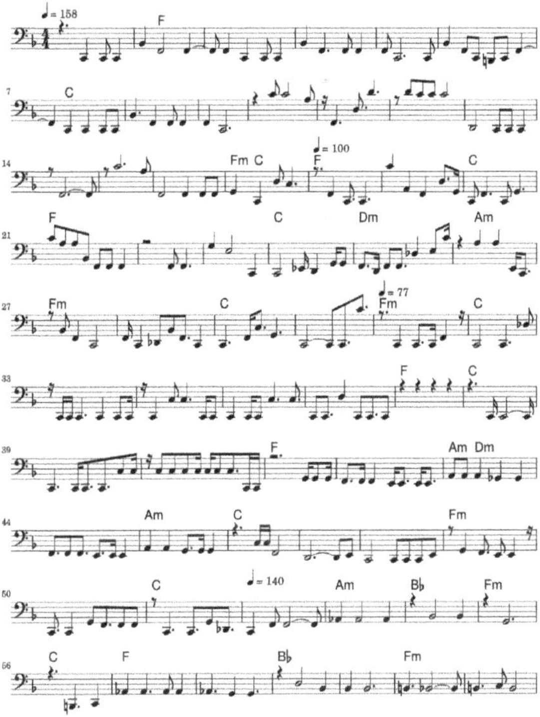

♩= 158
F
7
C
14
Fm C
♩= 100
F
C
21
F
C
Dm
Am
27
Fm
C
♩= 77
Fm
C
33
F
C
39
F
Am Dm
44
Am
C
Fm
50
C
♩= 140
Am
B♭
Fm
56
C
F
B♭
Fm

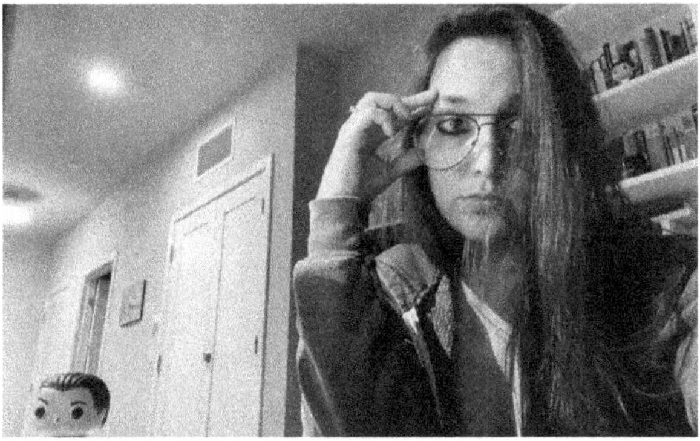

About the Author

Mallory Smart is a Chicago-based writer, editor-in-chief of Maudlin House, and doer of many other things.

Printed in the USA
CPSIA information can be obtained
at www.ICGtesting.com
LVHW090752181123
764187LV00004B/17

9 798987 478745